Epic Sloth

Tales of the Long Crawl

PHILIP GABER

ISBN: 0615726488
ISBN-13: 978-0-615-72648-9

Contents

"Nothing is funnier than unhappiness, I grant you that."
- Samuel Beckett

my forlornness caused me to lose track of time

There were things that were said that night, but I don't really remember.

I was either too drunk, too sleepy, or both.

The only thing I do remember is somebody got mad at me because I couldn't recall the name of the person they were describing.

"You know," the somebody said. "She has short, fleecy auburn hair, green eyes? Big-boned with a round, bland face?"

"I don't remember," I said.

"Yes you do!" the somebody said, nearly perforating my ear drums. "The one who uses a night light in her bathroom to look at herself in the mirror because she doesn't like the way she looks when she turns on the overhead light. She said it makes her face look like Morticia Adams!"

I shook my head.

"How can you not remember her? She was holding a jar of mayonnaise and dipping Doritos into it all night!"

"I don't remember!"

At that point, the somebody became so frustrated with me that they let out this little grunt and rolled their eyes and threw their hands up in almost total despair.

Actually, I thought their behavior was rather funny. I think I might have even snickered a little at them and I think they might have even heard me snickering at them, which only seemed to piss them off even more; although, as they sometimes say in the hood, I'm not a huned percent for sure.

The next morning, around 8:45, my cell phone rang.

I really didn't feel like answering it so I let the call go into my voicemail.

I went back to sleep and woke up an hour later.

As I was trying to figure out whether to have Lucky Charms or Froot Loops for breakfast, my cell phone rang again.

I looked at the caller ID.

The word "Private" was displayed.

I decided to hedge my bets.

"Hello," I said.

"It was Maude Love," a voice said.

"I'm sorry?"

"The person I was trying to remember last night. Her name was Maude Love."

"Who is this?" I said.

"Thelma!"

"Ohh, Thelma, hey..."

"I could not think of her name."

"Maude Love."

"Yess!"

I didn't remember anyone named Maude Love so I just kept my mouth shut. Because I knew Thelma. She'd start in on me again. About how I never listen to her or remember anything she tells me. Which I don't think is entirely true. It's just that she usually wants me to remember the things she wants me to remember, and I usually remember the things I want to remember.

"You remember Maude Love?" Thelma said.

"Uhmm..."

"You don't."

"Well..."

"Just say you don't," she said, frustrated as hell.

"I really don't," I said.

She didn't say anything after that. I was surprised. I figured she was going to take that opportunity to really lecture me on my active listening skills, but she didn't. Maybe she'd had it with lecturing me. Maybe I just wasn't a good enough student in her mismatched eyes. Who the hell knows?

Thelma ended the conversation the way she always ended our conversations by saying, "Well, anyway," which was my cue to say, "I guess I'll let you go."

But she'd always stay on the line for another minute or two, just breathing into the phone, and I'd turn on the TV and start flipping through the channels, waiting for her to say "goodbye", because I've always had trouble saying goodbye to Thelma. I'm really going to have to talk to my therapist about that someday.

Finally, she would whisper throatily "goodbye" and I'd be relieved, because then I could say goodbye, and we'd hang up, and I'd go to the kitchen, open the fridge, crack open a beer, sit there silently, lost in thought, hoping that one day the bright sun would bring my life to light.

a chronological complicated story

One morning Jenny and I were lounging around (I think it was a Saturday because Bugs Bunny cartoons were on) and she started talking all serious and stuff and wanting to know if I knew anything about the word commitment and if I did what it meant to me.

I recall lighting a cigarette and trying to stall a bit by humming a popular song of the day. Which really pissed her off. And then she said something like, "Well?" which was exactly the kind of thing my mother used to say to me whenever she caught me stalling.

I told her I had once read something John Adams said about commitment. "There are only two creatures of value on the face of the earth: those with the commitment, and those who require the commitment of others" and I asked her if that was the kind of commitment she was talking about.

She shook her head and rolled her eyes and made a weird hissing sound.

I didn't know what to say.

I mean, I knew what to say, I just didn't know how to say it.

Then she asked me one of those questions that make almost every guy like me squirm. "What do you want to do for the rest of your life?"

Questions like that can make you feel pretty down as soon as you hear it. Probably because it makes you realize how crappy your life really is. And it's doubly hard on a guy when a woman points out how crappy your life is. I don't know, it probably has something to do with our mothers; how we're always trying to please them. And how disappointed we are when we don't. Or can't.

Guys spend their whole lives trying to please women.

Well, guys like me, anyway.

I tried to think of a thoughtful, intelligent way of answering Jenny's question, but the only words that were forming in my mind were the kinds of words you shouldn't say in a situation like that. Words like, "I don't know," "I'm not really sure," "I haven't really thought about it, to tell you the truth."

And, anyway, when a woman hears words like that from a man, it's over for him. He might as well just thank her for a lovely relationship, pack his duffel bag and keep it moving. Because, if there's one thing I've learned about women, it's that most of them, I don't care how kind-hearted and caring they are, don't want to invest their time and energy in a stunted and plot-less guy. I don't care how desperate they are.

"Well?" Jenny said again.

Damn. Two "wells" in less than two minutes. That meant Jenny was really serious. Even my mom would limit her "wells" to every three or four minutes. Two "wells" from Jenny and I was beginning to wonder where my duffel bag was.

"Well," I said. Now I was saying it. Although my "well" probably had more to do with prolonging my adolescence than anything else. I mean, how the hell did she expect me to answer a question like that, anyway? How could anybody predict with any certainty *what* they would be doing in five *minutes* let alone fifty *years*?

"You're stalling again," Jenny said.

I had a few stock lines rattling around inside of me. "You deserve better," "It's not your fault, it's me," "I've lied," "I think we would be better off friends," "So long and thanks for all the fish," but I wasn't exactly looking to break up with Jenny. I mean I still loved her, as far as I knew. Didn't I?

"You're really that into me, heh?" I said. I know, it was even worse than any of those stock lines I'd sort of halfway considered.

She reacted pretty much like I expected. I didn't really understand everything she said because she was talking so fast, but none of it was good. Every now and then I'd recognize a word or a phrase. "Irresponsible and carefree", "a petulant and immature child-man", "aimless", "delaying adulthood..."

Really, if you want to know the truth, the only thing I remember were some of her facial expressions. Tense jaws, contorted eyebrows, wrinkles over the bridge of her nose, those kinds of things. I think she even started growling at one point, and that was a little weird. But I just let her vent. I figured eventually she'd get it all out of her system.

Twenty or thirty minutes later, I noticed her voice was getting a little hoarse. It sounded like she really could have used a nice cup of hot tea and honey. I think it would have soothed her vocal chords, but she gave no indication at all that she was at a point in her monologue where she could have stopped long enough to even enjoy a nice cup of hot tea and honey, so I just let her ramble on because I figured it would have only pissed her off even more if I was to interrupt her by asking her something as trivial as whether or not she'd like a nice cup of hot tea and honey to sooth her vocal chords.

I've learned to choose my battles.

Oh, an interesting thing happens to me whenever I'm being harangued by a woman. I fall asleep. I realize falling asleep is not exactly the most mature way of coping with conflict like that, and it certainly doesn't earn me any brownie points with anyone who's chosen to spend inordinate amounts of time with me, but I can't help myself. It started when I was a kid. And yeah, this anecdote does involve my mother, who seems to be popping up a lot in this story, much more than I intended, but I still think you'll get a kick out of it.

In 1976, I was eleven years old. And I had this habit of ignoring my mother whenever she'd ask me to do something like clean my room or vacuum the stairs or do the dishes or feed the cat or mow the lawn. As you can imagine, this kind of subversive behavior didn't sit too well with my mother. She actually considered it an act of deliberate betrayal. But instead of directly calling me on my shit, she'd go ahead and start doing whatever it was she'd asked me to do. I guess that was her way of trying to make me feel guilty, which it did, so I can't say her tactics were a complete waste of time, because I'd usually end up getting up off my ass at that point and completing whatever it was she was doing.

Then, on Saturday, July 3, 1976, around ten-o'clock in the morning, after I had just settled in to my favorite bean bag chair to watch reruns of Shazam and Isis, it happened. My mother became totally unhinged. I'm pretty sure it had something to do with all those acts deliberate betrayals. A mother can only take so many acts of deliberate betrayals from her children before she becomes psychotic with rage and verbally explodes.

It began when she asked me a simple question: "Did you empty the dishwasher?"

Of course, it was a question she already knew the answer to, which was another one of her tactics. I had to admit, though, for someone who already knew the answer to the question, she still put everything she had into asking it. My mother is that skilled of an interrogator.

Before I could even open my mouth to tell her I hadn't emptied the dishwasher, my mother began, quietly at first, to break down the meaning of the word procrastinate. It wasn't the first time she'd ever broken it down like that for me; but it was the first time she'd included the entire etymology of the word as well as the varying psychological causes associated with it.

Somewhere between her telling me that I might be suffering from a self-defeating attitude and a low sense of worth is when she really began to get stoked. And when I say stoked, I mean I actually heard her heart beating at one point. And I'd never seen her jaws clenched so tightly before; she probably could have used her entire face as a weapon, that's how pissed-off she was.

And that's when my dysfunctional little habit of falling asleep whenever a woman is yelling at me began.

The last thing I remember my mother saying before drifting off was, "What do you want to do, grow up to be a ditch digger?"

Anyway, long story short.

I fell asleep on Jenny and woke up about three hours later.

Naturally, she was gone.

A few minutes later, I got a text from her.

It said, "God puts people in your life to break your heart...not to hurt you but help you find that special someone."

I called Jenny and told her I'd never fall asleep on her again, because as far as I was concerned, she was that special someone, even though I didn't always tell her or show her. I told her I'd even drink a couple Red Bulls the next time she thought we should have one her "talks" so I'd be able to stay up long enough to actually hear whatever it was she wanted to tell me.

"If you think I'm so special, move out of your parents' house, go back to school. Wear something other than camouflage shorts and Red Hot Chili Peppers tee shirts because this is a you problem that has now become an us problem."

I said the only thing I could say at that point, which was, "Wow." And then thought the only thing I could think at that point, which was, *help*.

"Life is not just about how you feel inside," Jenny said. "It's what you evoke."

I could feel my eyelids getting heavy again and I wanted to close them and go to sleep, but I forced myself to stay awake.

"It's a simple choice," Jenny said, and she hung up.

I went into my bedroom, took two Vivarin, washed them down with a Mountain Dew, and began throwing out all my camouflage shorts and Red Hot Chili Peppers tee shirts.

It was the saddest day of my life.

some residue of character

Anthony's standing outside the Employment Security Commission Joblink smoking a cigar, drinking Aquafina. He's smiling this morning. Got a crick in his neck. "Musta slept wrong," he mutters. He's been unemployed for three months. Laid off from his job as a "tool and dye guy." Just turned forty. Just broke up with his girlfriend. "Just got paid by the Feds," he says with a crooked smile. "Uncle Sam's my Mister Charlie now." He's unsure of his future, though, says, "Some days I just don't give a shit. Other days I'm alright." Today, he says, he's alright. "Just had me a damn cheese omelet from The Waffle House. Those things are good? Mmmh."

His eyes are cloudy, has several scars on his face, "from the chickenpox." He's dressed in camouflage pants, a green t-shirt, Timberland boots, a leather choker. He thinks it's going to rain today, although he admits to not having heard a weather report in about six months.

A middle-aged woman wearing a scarf over her head and carrying a JC Penny bag gets off the city bus and walks toward Anthony.

"Where you been, boy?" she says.

"Girl, you don' wanna know," Anthony says, shaking his head, taking another drag from the cigar. "How you been?"

"Shooot," the woman says. "Day late and a dolla short."

Anthony nods.

The woman pulls out a pack of Newport Menthol Kings, tamps one out and puts it between her cracked lips.

Anthony lights the woman's cigarette.

"Wouldn't be so bad if somebody gimme a job," the woman says.

"Why you wanna job?" Anthony says, ironically.

"I dunno," the woman says. "Keeps me outta trouble."

The two are quiet for a moment, enjoying their tobacco and their down time.

Then Anthony says, "How's Andre?"

Andre is her only son. "Quit his job, moved out to Seattle," she says with a smirk.

"How come?"

The woman shrugs. "Be in a band, play in a band, doin' somethin' in a band. Boy's almost thirty-five years old…What is it with you men?"

Anthony smiles.

"Well, lemme get in here and see if I can't find me a job," the woman says.

"What kinda job you lookin' for?"

The woman puts her cigarette out in the ash tray. "Somethin' that don' wear me out," she says. "These old bones 'r' tiired."

"I heard that," Anthony says.

As the woman walks into the building, Anthony lights another cigar. He's decided not to knock himself out today, as he watches the parking lot begin to fill up with Lexus', Navigators, Escalades, Camrys, Accords.

He's still smiling, though.

It'll be alright, he thinks…It'll all be alright.

the state of

Godhead got a migraine.
Godfeet got corns.
Godhands got arthritis.
Godnose got a bleed.
Godear got tinnitus.
Godeyes got cataracts.
Godchest got a cold.
Godmouth got canker sores.
Gotheart god angina.
Godsoul got the blues.

he had a few things to sort out

I

I moved to L.A., played drums in a band, met a man named Itzhak Grossman, who said he'd discovered The Doors.

"Morrison was a drunk," he said. "Had issues with his mother. I came along and told him, you're a singer, sing. That shut him up."

Itzhak was a fraud, like so many. Always held court in his West LA digs. Denied his homosexuality. Preferred the company of wealthy, bed-ridden women who always found him "charming" and "gentlemanly". Wore silk shirts and scarves. Drank Dom Pérignon. Smoked Dunhills. Wore Rayban shades, even when it rained. Once showed me an autographed photograph of Andy Warhol. Later admitted to forging the signature during one of his infamous drinking binges.

"I'm looking for my fifteen minutes of fame, too, you know," he said. "I, of all people, deserve it."

One day Itzhak was found in his apartment by one of his short-time companions.

He'd hung himself using the leather laces from his ankle braces.

There was a note found on the coffee table that said, simply, "I was born. Now I'm sixty. God please have mercy on my poor soul."

II

They came by the half dozens in the rain to remember him.

As I was paying my respects, a young man in baggy jeans and a large diamond earring in one ear settled in next to me.

"He had a way of caressing you before breaking you," said the young man. "That was his aesthetic."

"Mmm," I said.

13

"When I first met him, I was kind of in a state of terror and confusion…and by week's end, I sort of started to enjoy it…I don't know what that says about my craziness or my sense of appetite."

"Hmm…"

"Did you know him well?"

"No," I said. "You?"

He weighed his response carefully. "We were a complicated couple…fire and fire makes more fire…always torn between what our hearts wanted and what our hearts needed. But, as they say, it's not whether you fall down, it's getting back up off the floor that matters…and, believe me, we saw a hell of a lot of floors."

The young man had to pause momentarily to bite down on his lower lip in order to keep himself from unraveling. "Excuse me, I'm sorry," he said, and he wandered toward the exit, leaving me alone.

I looked at my watch. I was late for my anatomy lesson with a lonely, fair-haired Chelsea Girl who had a glamour of her own and perfect posture.

Walking outside, I noticed the young man sitting cross-legged under a Dogwood tree, reciting a prayer. I heard him say the words "strength" and "honor" and the phrase "you never played chess with your life," and then he rose and disappeared around the corner.

III

It was just past noon when I arrived at my Chelsea Girl's townhome and after tasting her Shiraz-flavored lips, I felt something sweep out of me.

And in an instant, I became incredibly sick and almost blacked out, as my Chelsea Girl prepared to dissect my soul.

wrenched out of some familiar life-pattern

I never get the girl I like. I always get the gangly, angry girl with guileless eyes and stringy hair who has a tendency toward passivity. Or the gaunt, hyper girl with a nervous giggle and a brittle smile who is prone to sulking. Or the thin, vague girl with a black eye and a loud laugh who is terrified of clowns. Or the tiny, furtive girl with unruly hair and a bulbous nose who smells strongly of mothballs. he pudgy, depressed girl with a cleft chin and a silly grin who carries a concealed blade.

And then one day it dawned on me.

Maybe I never get the girl I want because I never became the man I was supposed to become. Because I wasted so many hours and days, even years, doing exactly the opposite of what I was supposed to be doing. Like smoking pot instead of doing my homework. Working as a dishwasher instead of going to college. Sleeping in instead of waking up. Fucking instead of committing. Committing instead of fucking. Drinking instead of not drinking. And I guess if you even wanted to toss a little psychology into all this mess you could probably explain away my behavior by saying something like people like me with weak social bonds are prone to self-destructive behavior, and I wouldn't argue with that, either.

Or maybe the reason is even simpler than that.

Maybe I unconsciously choose these girls just so I can reject them; because it's always easier to reject somebody if you don't like them, especially when you're rejecting them in order to get even with the multitudes who have rejected you because they didn't like you.

Could it be that?

Or maybe I'd just rather not be with anybody.

Maybe I prefer living a wistful, solitary lifestyle, in a dark one furnished room and kitchenette trying to remember when I was smiling, handsome, and young, and wasn't carrying around this burden of a sadness I can't seem to escape.

Could be that, too.

i've seen it ruin many a man

So now what?

Now that the press-on tattoos have all faded away and those twelve proof-of-purchases have been mailed off to Battle Creek, Michigan and we're no longer hung-over from that junior-high wine and we've phoned in our lives and we aren't sleeping and we look like we're forty and we're rubbing our temples and others are commenting on our restless souls and we no longer have moxie and naiveté and we're obsessed with our narcissistic nature and isolation?

What now?

where nothing else was growing

It was 1978.

They all wanted to know why I sat around drawing pictures of aliens and space ships and reading R. Crumb comics instead of studying or making friends or joining the Cub Scouts or Little League.

God forbid.

That's when the psychologists got involved. But they were frustrated by my shrugs, my I don't knows, and my lack of eye contact. Psychiatrists were strongly suggested, along with Ritalin, private schools, boot camps, religious instruction, extracurricular activities. My mother wanted to take away my drawing pad and my comic books. My father said if they took them away from me, then I'd really need a shrink.

So they left me alone.

And I started writing.

Today I still sit around writing and drawing pictures and reading comics and some people still wonder why I spend so much time doing those things and think I need to see a shrink.

Over the years I've learned to just smile and nod at these people and tell them how intuitive and insightful they are rather than argue with them.

Then I'll go home and write a story about them going to see a psychiatrist. And if they're lucky, I'll write a happy ending for them.

If not, I'll just end it like I end most of my stories. Unresolved and with an ellipsis at the end...

the artistic process is shady and subtle

I'd be off to the nearest bar drinking something the bartender had perfected in a test tube in the backroom where he saw mostly inside trading and poker faces and the occasional pot of gold at the end of a rainbow, which usually had a street value of about $140.73.

I'd drink and tell stories and jokes and smoke cigarettes rolled by brilliant lesbians and some nights I'd even get cored by scam artists from The Big Apple, but at least I'd have enough coin left over to rent a room for the night and buy a loaf of sprouted wheat bread and some meatless bologna and a bottle of wine made from grapes that were grown without the use of chemical fertilizers, pesticides, fungicides and herbicides.

Come morning, I'd head east or west, sometimes north or south, depending on my mood, and end up in a library or a church or an arcade or an amusement park; someplace where my failures weren't so noticeable.

I'd befriend a stray dog and name him after some Russian writer like Gogol or Turgenev or Pushkin and we'd travel sort of like Steinbeck and Charley, only I wasn't searching for America, just a clean, well-lit room where I could write and drink some wine and maybe even fall in love for at least an hour or two.

Eventually the mutt would grow weary of my aimlessness and my doubts and my lack of energy and dedication and wander off to some other part of the city where he could find a more symbiotic relationship.

I'd thread another page into my typewriter and try to figure out my childhood, but I'd always end up turning it into a fairy tale without a moral or a happy ending.

I'd regain consciousness the following morning, frustrated at the parameters linked to creation, and take my typewriter to a pawn shop, where a guy with frizzy blond hair, green eyes and a nervous giggle would loan me enough to keep me from becoming a hunger artist for a week or so.

Then I'd stroll over to the clinic and donate some of my blood plasma, strike up conversations with surly girls, gaunt sailors, naive prostitutes, and other well-meaning urban ghosts, collect my thirty-five dollars, cash the check at a liquor store, buy a bottle of brandy produced just outside the town of Cognac (because I was on a budget) and head to the sea, in search of waterfront women filled with primitive emotions and savage joys.

I'd buy them a gin and tonic and they'd say things like, "If I don't accomplish something of worth before my time is up, I'll start decaying before your very eyes."

By the third or fourth round of drinks, they would either be in tears or on the verge of proposing to me.

After their hangovers subsided, they'd rub their eyes and emerge from their reverie, realizing how little depth and dimension I'd added to their gray, silent lives, and say, "Guess a beautiful civil ceremony at city hall just wasn't in the cards for us," and I'd take them in my arms one last time, embrace them, and whisper something like, "I hope you shine through this world peacefully," and they'd leave, weeping, always weeping, while I continued to tramp the countryside alone, still believing in the myth of salvation, and hoping to gain some wisdom from my adventure, regardless of the outcome.

private paradise starting to fall apart

I shuffled the streets,
searching for sustenance,
pleading for redemption,
petitioning the world
for some compassion,
a small heroic gesture
of tenderness;
an arm around my shoulder,
a smile from a place
where the soul sometimes hides,
where the spirit resides,
but never subsides,
where joyrides
cause wide-eyed tie-dyed brides
to collide with the Ides of March,
forcing them to be pried
away from their pride and to
decide whether or not
the cry ever justifies the lie,
if the why is subtler
than the sigh,
if the I
is more important
than the my.

such a fine line between homage and plagiarism

Somebody once said writers are shameless sons-of-bitches filled with hubris. Or maybe they were just talking about Norman Mailer? I don't know. Anyway, I got a little lazy. My non-tenured writing instructor was telling me I needed to lay down a thousand words a day five days a week just to remain competitive.

I was stuck.

I'd taken a job at a drive-through cleaners making two hundred bucks a week and I was just too damn tired to sit down at the old Underwood and commit that kind of language to the page.

So I ended up taking a tape recorder to the streets with me.

I'd record whatever I could.

I would just let the tape roll.

Arguments, diatribes, monologues, didacticisms, laughter, tears, rambling, mumbling, cursing, petitioning, prayers, proposals, seductions, propositions, levity, brevity, serenity, insanity.

I was after something I couldn't create or recreate.

I was tired of my voice on the page; it sounded too much like my father and every other ne'er-do-well I knew.

It had become hoarse, course, full of remorse, everything I'd been fighting against since my undergraduate days at Ball State University, where I'd won a David Letterman scholarship for maintaining a C average.

What my writing teach didn't know wouldn't hurt her.

So I'd go to Washington Square Park in New York City, sit under a tree, light a Marlboro, turn on the recorder, and watch poverty and art having sex in public again.

anthem of a poignant reality

There are days when all those secrets and issues come back to me like a long, slow acid flashback.

There was something boldly experimental and oddly personal about me back then. The only way I can explain it is I was fearless. The reason I was fearless was because I had nothing to lose. The reason I had nothing to lose was because I had been less than nothing.

I was living by my heart and my mind and my wits and my passion. I'd developed a truth that mattered to me as much as anything I'd ever been involved in and I wanted to apply my intellect and strength to making the world a better place.

I spent the next twenty years playing the role of the semi-conscious hipster, chronicling the strong, beautiful, brutal violence of all those people that got burned by life and had to make up for bad decisions and lost time. And even though I thought I was being sensitive to the notion of the emotional complexities of what it was like to live in the world during that period, it was difficult for me to capture what was real vs. what I fantasized about.

So I stuffed most of those pages in a folder labeled *Yesterday's Cheap Thrills* and focused on what was selling in those days. Self-imposed angst, exploitation, lowbrow pulp, etc...

But no matter how inventive and honest I was, no matter how hard I worked at tweaking and amplifying the language in order to satisfy the aesthetic and thematic requirements of those clumsy submission guidelines, I could never get past those tricky, neon-light gatekeepers.

Maybe because there was too much pain and not enough art in those sad, silly stories.

Maybe because they didn't possess the kind of ecstatic beauty that causes most editors to experience multiple orgasms.

Or maybe because they just sucked.

I like to think that beneath all my noise I had moments that could be described only as exceptional, and a capacity and capability to do so much good.

And even if the only thing I'm remembered for is my encyclopedic knowledge of the angry and the marginalized, I still tried to sneak something heartfelt into the conversation every now and then and ask the mystifying and alluring question of whether or not under the persona was an ambitious man that worked diligently at hiding it.

Maybe the answer is finally in.

jet lag, loneliness and adrenalin

Wherever he went he drew brazen stares. Rebellious, uninhibited character. Never wanted more than a conquest, never told a girl he wanted to have a relationship when he didn't mean it. Always sounded nasally like he had a cold. Was having a lot of nosebleeds. His reaction to it was like it wasn't very serious. Dissolved cocaine in a glass of water and drank it. Didn't worry about drug-to-drug interactions.

Called up friends in the middle of the night: "I love you and if you don't love me, I'm sorry."

White Corvette convertible was his dream. Teal Chevy Celebrity was his nightmare. Succeeded in calming himself only after reading about the Mormons. IRS problems. Two hundred dollar a day heroin habit. Drank sake bombers. Then the phone stopped ringing. Has-been at twenty-two. Deeply despondent. Frantically sough to exit a dead-end road. Trapped in a vicious cycle. Looked for some way out. A tearful goodbye. Became a specialty act. Knees bruised and bloodied from too much groveling. Writing checks to get his dog out of the kennel. Desperation deepened. "Sometimes I wish I could just blow my brains out," he told his phone therapist. Wild mood swings.

Going down the stairs, had a bottle of wine in his hand, hopped into his teal Chevy Celebrity, in a rush to go home to Mom. Had no intention of slowing down. Hit a curve at high speed. Plowed into a tree. Steered the Celebrity into Mom's driveway. Into the garage. Nose broken.

"Head. . . hospital..."

Inconsolable. Laying on the floor of the Celebrity, legs spread, 9 mm pistol between his legs, looking at his reflection in some shards from the rear view mirror. POP! All this blood. Pool of blood. The wound looked like this big flower on the side of his head.

you can use vitamins to help a woman through those things

She wore a white Sapphire ring. Chain-smoked herbal cigarettes. Always blew smoke rings. She'd sit at her desk, mumbling to herself, "Wonder how much I should take…Let's see, what would I do in that situation?…Ooh, my mouth hurts…"

If you thought she was talking to you and you asked her to repeat herself, she'd say, "Oh, nothing, I'm just talking to myself. Pay me no mind. Very few people do, anyway," then chuckle in a self-deprecating way and continue doing whatever it was she was doing at the moment, which was usually nothing very interesting: sharpening a pencil, doodling on a paper towel, playing Mine Sweeper on her computer.

Very occasionally you'd find her doing something useful, like washing her car, practicing her interviewing skills in front of a fun house mirror, studying the bus routes.

I met her just after she had been released from the country jail for doing something she would never talk about. Knowing her, it probably had something to do with driving while intoxicated or assaulting an ex-boyfriend with a deadly weapon, but that's just a guess.

If you looked directly into her eyes, her lashes would flutter; she'd experience innate anxiety and begin quoting from nature shows. "As amphibian ancestors emerged from primeval lakes and seas to live part of their lives on land, seeing and hearing sharpened."

During one of her quieter moments, you might hear her reveal something like, "Lot of beer, lot of truck stop speed, lot of pot…I just don't remember a lot of my first marriage," then see her cast her eyes toward a doorway or a window, and release her breath, which always smelled of toothpaste.

If you happened to catch her recovering from a particularly intense orgasm, she might whisper into your ear, "Ohmygodohmygod, I think I might have a cyst on my brain," or "I need quiet, peace, tranquility, you know what I mean," and then drift off to sleep, always muttering something wild and foul.

She might have been the last of the blue, cold lovers.

I don't know.

She never asked you to do anything illegal or immoral, but if she ever lost focus around you, she'd start speaking in non sequiturs or laughing at your fractured syntax or reminiscing about her "Steely Dan Period."

Then one day she went away on an unexpected hiatus.

Some say she became a missionary to Ecuador's Auca Indians.

Others say she ran off to Italy to work as a cobbler.

But I think she just became bored of being one person on Monday and another on Tuesday and of constantly having to play the role of the eager blonde pretending not to have the personality to do tragedy and she just had to disappear.

woke up without a hangover

I shower, shave, shovel a couple eggs down my throat, worry about losing my job because my manager thinks I'm "unconventional and withdrawn," and don't "follow through enough."

I shrug through my coffee, cover my body with the same blue Oxford shirt and tan khaki pants I wore the day before and probably the day before that, hobble out the door with bad breath and no breath mints and a definite sense of schlub.

My sky blue Skylark is my friend this morning. It starts. On the first try.

However, halfway down the street I run over a nail.

And I don't have the kind of tires that can run over a nail.

I have the kind of tires that can barely run over a road.

My life's quota of flat tires has not been met.

So my sky blue Skylark limps to the shoulder, where it must lean for now.

reborn

Mayor Majeskie invited anyone wishing to speak during the open forum
to step forward and that's when Briana came forth and said, "Not that I'm
hatin on you but you're thinkin my job is to placate you and I'm thinkin
my job is to vacate you. I've seen the sit-ins and the back of the busses,
seen the front of the busses, too, and the view ain't no better up there. I've
read Marcus and Malcolm and Langston and Lorraine and Ralph and
Martin and James and Maya and Toni and came to the conclusion that all
them words just gimme a damn headache. I now know why so many white
folk got such a thrill outta watchin *Roots*, and I've made love to Kunte Kinte
a million times and been his bride at least as many times. I've cried for
Dorothy and Josephine and Billie and Hattie and Butterfly McQueen and
I've paid my debt to jungle fever and given birth to children who will pass.
I've witnessed The Lord first, second and third hand and seen his miracles
whip us into a frenzy, but don't have a clue why He ain't given us our peace
of heart yet. Forgive me, Malcolm, forgive me, Martin, but I'm still alone,
still fighting, still shackled, still in love, but still confused. My color, my
content, my character has survived, but at what point will I know when I've
truly arrived? Affirmative action keeps me educated, but so what, I'm the
only Person of Color in the Humanities Department. My brothers, my
sisters all assume I'm a token, simply because I'm so well-spoken. I'm alive,
I will survive, and I sure enuf ain't no midwife. With or without you, I will
never be all about you, and as long as your tongue keeps me from climbin
your rungs, I will be content to be your worst malcontent 'cuz my intent
is to put a dent in your pent-up guilt and watch your ego wilt. Share that,
Majeskie."

And as the City Clerk prepared to submit Mayor Majeski's resignation,
City Councilor Earnest Belliveau said "And on that note, I request
adjournment."

i wanna make an art-house film for an art-house crowd

I wanna make an art-house film for an art-house crowd.

There'll be no emotional climax and it won't reach a clear conclusion.

It'll be a fractured story of a man and a woman and their ideas will clash against one another like two hearts stored in a store-bought cooler battling for the chance to be transplanted into the body of an whiny billionaire.

Their relationship will endure many months of awkwardness and strong undercurrents of tension and sadness and anger and eventually they will each learn too late the folly of clinging to defensive illusions.

It'll premier at the Sundance Festival, where it will begin to gain popularity.

The New York Times will say my art-house film for an art-house crowd is "intellectually stimulating" and "aesthetically bold" and one of my aspiring something or other friends will say it's more poignant and less reliant on the tired tricks and predictable posturing than any of my previous films and I'll nod meaningfully and thank them.

It'll be distributed on a limited basis to a few art-house friendly venues across the country; however it will not enjoy a particularly successful theatrical run largely because of its "cerebral experience" which will ultimately mean I won't not be able to move out of my spartan apartment above my parent's garage into that small bungalow where the trees and shrubs are strategically planted to block the view of my neighbors like I originally planned.

a very earnest liberal lady from westchester

She has knowledge stored for a future use. Rooms are generally quiet and respectful while in her presence. After becoming engaged, she began hyperventilating on a regular basis and her skin mottled.

When someone asked to see her engagement ring, she excused herself and got sick in the ladies room, and told the bathroom attendant, "I need love and comfort and space to breathe."

"Girl, you know men are like food," the attendant said. "You're lookin' for a hunka raw meat and gettin' a lumpy bowl a oatmeal."

When she awoke the following afternoon, she made a daring escape, took a risk, and listened to her own sense of style and made sure that anything that could possibly help her was far away from her.

on this very troubled afternoon

Between summer's mist and winter's rain,
the faceless, voiceless mourners
recede into yesterday's succor,
engulfed in the waves which soar above the sand.

"The graveyard's threshold opens
and we step toward its eddying silence,"
the incurious minister says,
peering into another wandering void.

Light white rain descends in the dark clear shade
as the mother's ultramarine eyes glance
at the silver white edge of a raindrop,
her blue white tears moistening her black veil.

The sparkling childhood ring she holds in her hand
will one day shine again in the sun's clear white song.

that well hung-over look

My prose was flaccid, a little crass, lacked clarity and structure. My characters were about as developed as a third world country and my analogies were as sophisticated as a bottle of Manischewitz Extra Heavy Malaga wine.

So I holed myself up in an old saltbox house in New Hampshire. Gained weight, discovered Zen Buddhism, Marxism, and punk rock. I was searching for an identity. Anyone could see that. But I was so charming about it, most people forgave me.

When I finally got the courage to begin writing again, this was the only thing I could come up with:

"I'd always been a little behind with losing my baby teeth. In fact, my last tooth came out in 7th grade. First period English. We were watching a movie. I worked that molar until POP! Out it came. I placed it in a napkin and left it behind."

It was gone. My facility for language. For forming ideas that assaulted the imagination and offended Goths at open mike nights. The gardens had all turned to weeds and the seeds had moved on to more fertile soil.

I went into the kitchen, fixed myself a bowl of Cream of Wheat and folded in some Grape Nuts and a sliced banana and drizzled some honey over it.

I recalled my final conversation with my father, in which he called my friends "moral degenerates, dope heads, drunks, and psychopaths."

Ironically, it was on All Saints' Day, which was fitting, considering we were both martyrs.

9/11

A flag was raised
and the pope put his hand to his forehead.
An old man cried into a bouquet of flowers
and candles stayed lit on a sidewalk.
A young woman kept feeling her stomach
and a street musician injected a bit of humor into his veins.
A fireman coughed
and somebody up on a cross
made an effort to exaggerate the lies
that had been told to him since he was an embryo.

so many quiet spots in our lives

You told me you grew up in a foster home. Fantasized about being adopted by that anguished young couple you saw from your bedroom window on that chill New Year's Eve morning.

The husband, smoking, shaking his head and looking at his wristwatch, stood stiffly.

The wife, silent and sullen, arms folded, eyes shielded by sunglasses, paced the parking lot.

But you decided he was too short to be your father and she was too hard-looking to be your mother, so you scrapped the whole idea.

Then suddenly you looked at me and said, "I'm sorry. I gotta go."

"Wha?" I said.

"I'm not in a very good place these days."

"What are you talking about?"

"I can't do this…I'm sorry…Love is…not what I'm interested in at the moment…We'll only end up imploding…"

"Imploding?"

"My foster mother told me, with men you've got to be loving, adoring, and forgiving. And I…am none of those things."

"But we made plans," I said. "We were gonna move to Santa Barbara. You were gonna open up a little rare bookshop. I was gonna find myself. What happened?"

"All I can say is, I have no idea what to say. Let's just stick a fork in it and call it a day."

You held out your hand and wished me a great life.

Instinctively, I offered my hand, but I was so stunned, it just sort of dangled there and we never did shake hands.

You reached into your purse, took out a bottle of aspirin, popped three of them in your mouth and chased them with some coffee.

"It's all good," you said. "Everything's good."

That night I walked to that all-night diner where we'd first met and had a piece of key lime pie. I felt like I was coming down with a fever so I went into the bathroom to splash some cool water on my face.

I avoided the mirror completely; I wasn't ready to confront that look of heavy resignation beginning to form around my eyes.

I went back to my table, pulled out my wallet, laid down a ten and left.

this fully-human existential predicament

Angus Chitty took an old Underwood typewriter to Madison Square Park, sat down on a bench and began typing:

```
The focus had shifted from liberation and fun and
excitement to how downtrodden and miserable
everybody's lives had become.
```

That's when some film students from the local school of visual arts approached him and asked him if he wanted to be in their thesis film.

"What's it about?" Angus said.

A tall, skinny kid with Jesus hair and an Iggy Pop tee shirt spoke.

"It's about this scientist who invents this technology whereby you have the ability to pick and choose which brain cells you wanna kill off while you're drinking or doing drugs…'cuz, ya know how like you lose a thousand brain cells every time you take a drink or smoke a joint, yet have absolutely no control whatsoever over which cells die? Well, this technology enables you to actually choose with pinpoint accuracy, man. Say, for instance, you wanna knock off high school algebra. You hook these little electrodes up to you before you start partying and you program the computer to knock off, let's say, high school algebra or that recent date with a tranny, whatever it is you wanna whack. That way you get to hold on to the cells you really wanna keep, ya know?"

"I'll do it," Angus said.

Jesus hair nodded coolly, handed Angus his business card, and told him to call him.

"I'm 'onna need you to shave your head and lose about fifteen pounds," Jesus hair said.

Angus nodded. "What part am I playing?"

"Got a couple of parts in mind. One of 'ems an ironic hardcore gay rapper. The other's an alcoholic school bus driver struggling with career-choice issues. I think you'd be perfect for both."

"Thanks," Angus said.

And the film students walked off into the sunset, leaving Angus Chitty to worry about how he was going to shed fifteen pounds in such a short amount of time.

Tearing the page from the typewriter, Angus neatly folded it into an airplane and flew it toward some pigeons that were snacking on an old sandwich.

Wow, dreams always come at such a high price, Angus thought as though nobody had ever thought that thought before.

He loaded another blank page into the typewriter and typed:

```
I used to know what women thought: "This is the
face that people want." I used to know what men
thought: "I want to be somebody soon." Now all I
know is this: that life is a more unusual problem
for a man and a woman to have than I originally
thought.
```

day of reckoning

You're always on the hot seat whenever you're not doing what the rest of the world is doing.

It's never easy.

Fear and anxiety are always just around the corner, smiling behind your back, taunting you, determining your fate with the toss of a coin.

"Heads or tails, brother, heads or tails. . ."

You choose heads, it's always tails. You choose tails. . .

You get the idea.

On the surface, it all seems harmless. But underneath it all, it's a chess match. Only without an end game. And without any queens or knights or rooks or horses. Just pawns and the occasional castle where the kings reside.

Inevitably, the game ends in a stale mate and both players go home, attempting to design new chess pieces, inventing new strategies; but their consciences won't allow it, nor will the rules.

So they carve their initials into the remaining pieces and hope that the kings allow them to share the castle before the pawns rise up and shout, "Check mate!"

thorn in the lover

I woke up this morning and thought about what you said the other day; how you hoped I wouldn't turn out to be like all those other guys. Like Reginald Lukas who only smiled whenever somebody said "Cheese!" Or Takeuchi Hidemichi who smelled like he owned a fish hatchery. Or Crispin Dumont who lived in a motel room near Highway 61. Or Louis-Sebastien Aubert who kept insisting he was an "entrepreneur." Or Charlie Crowder who just liked to sit on a park bench all day long. Or Mike McGahan who played the ukulele in the nude. Or Leonard Lagrand who drank all day and played solitaire all night. Or Laszlo Roskam who said he was the saddest son-of-a-bitch you'd ever want to meet. Or Manny Malkoff who believed he was going to be the next something or other. Or Florian Schultz who was always falling down and breaking some bone in his body. Or Mohammad Lawson who only said his prayers when he was in front of a judge.

I thought about all those guys and tried to figure out why you'd even *think* I'd be anything like them.

Is it because I prefer to be alone on Christmas, writing poetry? Because my New Year's resolution is to read the entire works of Dr. Seuss? Because I still eat Chef Boyardee and Cap'n Crunch cereal? Because I like to play my Djembe African drum in the middle of the night? Because I observed Holy Communion during last year's Passover Seder? Because I wear brown shoes with a tuxedo? Because I haven't outgrown *The Catcher in the Rye*? Because people often describe me as being "wild" and "unkempt?" Because I never walk in a straight line? Because I like to drink with the winos on Portrero Hill? Because of my obsession with movies that contain graphic violence and biblical themes?

I guess I should probably just ask you the next time I see you, heh? Instead of writing this on the back of a cocktail napkin?

Alright, then, I'll do that.

you just can't keep track of the turns in the road

The man with the beard down to his heart roams the hallways of Pine Meadow Elementary School as an Indian leg wresting tournament takes place in the gymnasium.

Several reporters mill about the school grounds, awaiting the outcome of their human interest story, smoking Pall Malls and hitting from flasks filled with Kentucky bourbon.

A frail, elderly woman, walking with a cane, enters the building, muttering something about Medicare, her children in Cleveland, and her estranged husband, who's an Atheist and a registered Communist.

A boy and girl in the first grade have one of the most in-depth conversations of their lives:

"You get inside a tea cup and it spins you round and round," the girl says.

"Is it fun?" the boy says.

"Yessss! I loved it!"

"I wanna go!"

"Ask your mommy and daddy to take you. I think it probably only costs about seventy or eighty dollars."

A teenager, dressed to unimpress, listens to Ozzy on an iPod, sings off-key about a crazy train, wishes he could play the guitar like Randy Rhodes, while an underperforming car salesman sits in his car in the parking lot of the school reminiscing about his childhood and inhaling a baloney and American cheese sandwich with spicy mustard and Miracle Whip on Wonder bread, just as he did thirty years ago.

The reporters extinguish their cigarettes by grinding them into the grass with their feet.

"What did the NASDAQ close at yesterday?" one of them asks.

"Don't follow it," someone answers.

Meanwhile, the children in the gymnasium cheer wildly as their peers engage in what one teacher sarcastically describes as "a real team-building experience."

But the children don't understand sarcasm yet. They know nothing of irony or the walls we write on or the lines we read between. Their minds are fresh, unfettered, clown-like in their depth.

The elderly woman with the cane enters the administrative office, requesting to pick up her grandson, who attends school in Cleveland.

"Could you page him for me, please?" she asks the school secretary.

"What's his name?"

The elderly woman thinks for a minute. "I can't remember. Are we in Cleveland?"

"No, ma'am. Connecticut."

"Oh, lord. I've done it again."

Outside, the car salesman motions for the teenager listening to Ozzy to come over to his car.

"Do you remember the laughter?" says the salesman.

The teenager laughs, lights a Marlboro Light. "Dude, you're wasted," he says, walking away.

"What happened to me?" says the car salesman.

The teenager twists around and says, "You gave up on yourself, brah…"

Inside, the Indian leg wrestling champ of Pine Meadow Elementary School is jumping up and down, wildly waving his hands.

"THE WORLD IS MY OYSTER!" he shouts.

He's presented with a gold-plated medal, engraved with the inscription:

1973 Indian Leg Wrestling Champion
Pine Meadow Elementary School

The challenger, as instructed by his gym teacher, shakes the champ's hand, and is awarded with a silver-plated medal, engraved with the runner-up inscription. The gym teacher pats the challenger on the butt and says, "Way to go! Good job, buddy! Way to go!"

The two boys stand awkwardly, joining opposing hands, raising them above their tiny heads like miniature presidential candidates.

Outside the car salesman sheds a tear, cranks the ignition, and drives back to work, as the elderly woman passes the man with the beard down to his heart, and says, "Have you seen my grandson?"

He looks at her and says, "Nana?"

the hardest victory

The aged actor accepted his lifetime achievement award.

"When you use that word 'Legendary'," he said. "It usually refers to somebody who is very old or very deceased."

It got a decent-sized laugh.

About the size of a 10 ½ double D pair of loafers.

Then, leaning against the podium, and obviously drunk, he pointed a finger into the camera and said, "Lissen, I gotta few things I'd like to get off my chest…This is such a smarmy business we're in…I mean, let's face it, we lie to you every chance we get…This entire business is a canard…and what is so utterly inconceivable to me is that you *continue* to believe our lies…You're smarter than that…Is it that our lies are so much more damn interesting than the lies you tell yourselves?…Why the hell should you even care about us? We don't care about you. What the hell have we ever done that's so goddamn terrific? Nothing! *Nothing!*"

Suddenly his mike went dead.

However, the camera stayed on him.

And if you knew how to read lips, you would have seen them say, "I'm a goddamn drunk, but you know what? I'm not ashamed…I'm tired of people being ashamed of drinking! Christ, drinking enhances my pride, my dignity, my integrity! I feel like God Almighty Himself when I'm drinking!"

That's when somebody in the control room screamed for somebody else to cut to the nebbish host of the ceremony, who had a look of perverse fascination. "Wow, talk about your feet of clay," the host quipped.

Then everything went black and quiet and suddenly the local news anchor appeared. "A new study by researchers reveals that a lot of jerks drive luxury vehicles. Details at eleven."

untitled

I'm currently working on a novel
based on a synopsis of an idea
inspired by a word in a sentence
developed from a feeling of an image I experienced
as a result of a memory I had as a child.

the secret of her bloom

I auditioned for an off-off Broadway production titled "A Widow from Montclair" written by a sixty-four year old dentist, recently retired, who was now pursuing a career as a playwright. When I finished reading my prepared monologue, the director whispered something to the dentist and the dentist nodded approvingly. I couldn't quite grasp the fact that the guy was a playwright, so in my mind, I kept referring to him as "The Dentist."

"We'd like you to read with the male lead," the director said, looking around. "Where's Dennis?"

"He went to Starbucks. He said he'd be right back," said a voice from the rear of the theater.

The director sighed. It sounded like he muttered, "Jesus Christ," but I wasn't sure. He took off his glasses, rubbed his face with his hands, shook his head and muttered again. Then the dentist whispered something to the director, who snickered, as if someone had included him in a very obscene joke.

"Dennis is back!" said the voice from the rear.

In walked Dennis, sipping something hot from Starbucks. He was wearing khaki shorts, an unbuttoned Hawaiian shirt over a white tee shirt and leather flip flops. He looked to be in his mid to late thirties. His hair was receding and he wore the rest of it in a ponytail.

"Yo!" Dennis said.

"Dennis, want you to read with Molly," the director said.

"Absolutely!"

"Act two, scene four."

"Solid!"

Dennis motioned for the stage manager to toss him a copy of the script, which he immediately dropped as soon as it reached him. "I can do this," he said, bending over to pick up the script. "I am a professional."

As Dennis approached me, he winked and gave me a half smile and then produced one of those noises people sometimes make when giving orders to a horse.

"Hey, Molly, Dennis Filcher, pleasure to meet'cha. Let's do this sucker… when you're ready."

I turned to act two, scene four.

The scene called for Dennis to be tossing a cigarette on the ground, stamping it out with his foot, and then dropping to the floor for a series of push-ups. "'Well, I think your scars are very deep, Maggie,'" Dennis said, already practically out of breath. "'I believe in healing. I think that you're doing fine. But, I think, periodically, things creep up, insecurities. I think it's… I think it's a case of, if the dog hadn't stopped to pee, he might have caught the rabbit.'"

I let out a big sigh because that's what the stage directions said to do, but I really wasn't feeling the audition. I was about to say the hell with the whole thing and get my ass out of there when the director suddenly lurched out of his chair and shouted, "Yesss! Yesss! That's brilliant! That is exactly what I'm looking for!"

I just looked blankly at him.

"You have such an incredibly angry, suppressed sort of totally tragic cheekiness about you, which I find absolutely irresistible."

"Thanks," I said, adding, "But I didn't even get a chance to say my first line."

"Who did you study with?" the director said.

"Uhm…myself?"

The director laughed manically. "Girl, you're a trip. You've got the part. Congratulations."

"Thanks," I said, sort of blasé.

Dennis made that horrible horse noise again and extended his hand. "Great job, Molly," he said. "You rocked the hell out of that thang."

I shook his hand and bowed my head for some stupid reason. Ordinarily, I'm not in the habit of bowing my head whenever somebody compliments me. In fact, I think it was probably the first time I'd ever bowed my head to anyone in my life. It was especially upsetting knowing I'd done it to a schmuck like Dennis, who was so totally undeserving of a head bow to begin with.

"How 'bout we do dinner later?" he said.

"I can't. I have Bible study tonight."

"Oooh, Bible study," he said with a subtle sneer. "Interesting. Well I'd really like to sit down with you sometime and talk about your process."

"My process?"

"Your approach to the craft."

"Ahh, my approach. Well, my approach is very simple. Just say the lines and don't bump into the furniture."

Dennis laughed. He had one of those loud, embarrassing laughs that made you never want to say anything funny to him ever again. He didn't even realize I had borrowed the bump into the furniture line from Spencer Tracy, which meant I was forced to take major cool points away from him, which left him with a really negative score.

"Boy, you're gonna be a blast to work with," he said.

"I'm really looking forward to this," I lied.

Then he leaned forward and whispered, "Listen, don't let Mark intimidate you. This is his first stage production. He's been directing some kids show on Nickelodeon or the Disney Channel or some shit for the last five years. He's not used to working with real actors."

"Thanks," I said. "That helps me a whole lot."

"Dennis! I need you!" the director shouted.

"Coming," Dennis said. "Always coming!" He patted me on the shoulder and winked. "And I do mean, always coming."

I waited for him to do the horse noise again, but thank God he didn't.
As I walked out of the theater, I thought, what the hell am I about to sign on for here?

Two weeks before the show was supposed to open, Dennis withdrew for personal reasons and the role couldn't be reassigned so late in the rehearsal process, so they had to cancel the production. I was so furious with him that I called him.

"Dennis, what the hell is wrong with you?"

"I just feel like I'm surrounded by people who are totally unconcerned with my spiritual well-being," he said.

I slammed the phone down and screamed.

Thirty seconds later the phone rang.

"Hello?" I said.

It was Dennis.

"Man, you're a lot of work," he said.

I slammed the phone down again, this time taking it off the hook. I had such a volatile cocktail of emotions raging inside of me that I began to scream wildly, pounding the arm of the couch with my fists until some of my knuckles were bruised and bloody. I would never forgive Dennis for what he did to me! To us! Granted, the play was astoundingly neurotic and self-indulgent, and imperfectly written, but it was *work!* Now I'd have to schlep down to the unemployment office and play *that* fecocta game again! Christ, *I've* been "surrounded by people who were totally unconcerned with my spiritual well-being," my entire *life!* You don't see *me* "withdrawing for personal reasons" two weeks before the fucking show opens!

I sunk into the couch, and closed my eyes. I was in such a paralyzing stupor, I just sat there for the next forty-five minutes staring at all the paint runs, bumps, dents and grit on my walls.

When I finally fell asleep, the sun's light was all up in my face.

Later that day, I went to my gynecologist. I told her I thought I might be depressed.

"It can be just that, your progestin levels, your hormones get out of whack," she said. "And then it sucks your cortisol level and then your cortisol level makes you puffy and fat, so you're depressed. Simple as that."

"Is it really as simple as that?" I asked her.

She smiled and nodded. "You're fine."

I noticed a cactus sitting in a pot on the counter next to the sink. It looked like it was beginning to rot and seemed to be melting into the dirt. "Your cactus is dying," I said.

"Mm hm," she said, reviewing my records.

"Maybe you can take some cuttings and root them."

"Mm hmm."

She scribbled something in my records, closed my file, stood up, and extended her hand. "Everything looks great," she said.

"Great," I said, shaking her hand, and I left.

When I got back to my apartment, there was a message on the answering machine from Dennis apologizing for his "self-indulgent behavior." He went on to say that he thought he might be battling with undiagnosed cases of attention-deficit hyperactivity disorder, panic disorder, and manic depression and maybe it was time he finally confronted his demons and entered into therapy.

"My life just feels like a lot of effort with zero payoff," he said. "Guess it's time to reassess my life mission."

That's when the answering machine cut him off.

I envisioned Dennis, completely smashed on two wine coolers, totally oblivious to having just been disconnected, still talking into the phone four hours later, disclosing all of his psychic scars.

"Just don't turn psycho stalker on me, brother," I said.

I erased his message, grabbed a Bud Lite from the fridge, sat down on the couch, turned on Home and Garden TV, and got comfortably buzzed.

Before the host of the program could fully explain how to propagate roses, I was asleep and dreaming I was a little hothouse orchid, exotic and touchy, and unprotected from the sun.

a persistent illusion

Ohh lemme tell you, I ran into Ronny Halberstan. Remember Ronny?

Noo.

Guy who put up some of the seed money for my club.

Okay?

Guy is strung out on h.

Really?

Ohh. He's about ninety pounds, looks like an Auschwitz survivor. Gave him twenty bucks, told him to go get a sandwich or something. He won't. He'll use it for drugs. But my God, I didn't even recognize him. He approached me. Can you imagine what it took for him to do that? I know he lost a boatload on some internet stocks. I mean he's always had his demons, they go very deep, you know, he was always a depressed sorta character, always on the verge of suicide, never knowing where he stood with men or women. I'm not knockin' him for it 'cause the guy obviously needs help.

Right.

My point is, how does a guy who had so much potential and so much talent succumb to that sort of a breakdown?

I have no idea.

Guy went to Harvard, for Chrissakes.

People are very complex, Mel.

Now I kinda feel bad just flippin' him a twenty…maybe I shouldda…Whaddaya think? Should I have intervened more than I did?

It's hard to say.

What would you have done?

Probably exactly what you did.

I mean, it's not like we were friends or anything. He was the money guy. I knew him very superficially, we never even socialized. Quite frankly, I thought he was a pain in the ass, but who the hell am I?

I don't know what to tell you, Mel.

The guy had no shame at all about coming up to me. Like the continuity of our association had never been broken.

Where'd you see him?

The airport, of all places. Joanie's father's sick, he has the first stages of pancreatic cancer, so she flew out. I was dropping her off…What the hell was *Ronny* doin' there, though? That's *my* question. I'm leaving the terminal, I hear this voice. "Mel!" I turn around, I'm starin' at this bag o' bones tryna to get a read on his face thinking, "Who is this guy?" He says, "It's Ronny," he says. "Ronny? Jesus Christ, that's you?" He says, "Yeah, how ya doing?" I was so blown away. You know I never think about what I say half the time, I say a lot of stupid shit. I say, "Ronny, Jesus, what happened to you?" And he goes into this whole long drama about being hooked on the h and everything…and I'm standing there with my jaw on the floor thinking, this guy used to be like an Adonis! He was a bodybuilder, for Chrissakes! …My first instinct was to reach into my wallet and give him a twenty, I dunno why, I guess I was nervous, I couldn't even look at him, I mean, it was painful to look at him, I didn't know what the hell else to do. What should I have done? What else should I have done?

I don't know, Mel.

It's nuts, right?

That's life.

I know but it's crazy.

I know it's crazy.

Should I have done more?

Whaddaya gonna do?

I don't know. I suppose I could've left my number with him.

What's he gonna do with your number?

In case of an emergency, I dunno.

How involved do you wanna get? You wanna perform an intervention on him? Check him into rehab? Pay for his rehab? How far do you take it? And do you trust him? You did the right thing...

I feel like I owe him something, though.

What do you owe him for? For giving you a portion of the seed money for that club of yours? He got his money back, didn't he?

Yeah.

So what do you owe him?

I dunno.

Well, if you don't know, then you probably don't owe him anything.

I dunno, he sorta haunts me.

He *haunts* you?

The image of him standing in the terminal haunts me. He looked like he had the collective pain of mankind on his face. I know it's nuts, I can't explain it, but I've been having nightmares about the guy. His face. His emaciated body. Two of his teeth were missing. Oh, he had such an odor, he smelled of death. I dunno what the hell death smells like, but I'm sure he smelled like it. It was nauseating. And he had these lesions on his neck.

Maybe he's got A.I.D.S.

I dunno what the hell he's got...I'll tell you, though, it scared the hell outta me. You know what it was like? It was like in *A Christmas Carol* when Marley comes back and tells Scrooge whatever the hell he tells him. It was like that. So you're thinking I'm cool. I don't need to...call him or follow up with him or anything.

Why, because he haunts you?

No, you're right. Leave it alone…

it was a rare moment when i had almost everything i wanted

It was Thanksgiving morning. Mid-morning to be exact. I remember it just like it was four years ago Thursday. I awoke, amazingly. Although for the life of me I couldn't remember what I'd dreamt. The first thing I did, which is what I'd always done, and continue to do to this day, was drink a shot of Kentucky bourbon. I've tried North Dakota bourbon, and I'm sorry, it's just not the same. It was so delicious, I had another shot. Because, quite frankly, what else was there to do? Oh sure, I could have read a self-improvement book or enrolled in a continuing education program at the local community college or wrote a poem or turned to religion or smoked some opium or got married or laughed at a joke or wandered through the desert like my ancestors; but Kentucky bourbon just has a way of exerting its ownership over men like me and I guess there's a part of me that loves how it feels to be dominated. And I'm not ashamed to say it.

Several minutes later, I got a call from a woman who always smelled of cocoa butter. Her name was Marjorie; and she claimed to be born under a morning star.

"I'm feeling off-kilter," she said.

"When was the last time you felt on-kilter?" I said.

"April…or May." She then let out a primal scream. "Sorry," she said. "Must have experienced some childhood trauma and repressed it. So how are you, my lust?"

"Feeling somewhat anachronistic," I said. "Been sleeping with friends on couches and floors…was arrested for drunkenness and vagrancy…other than that…"

Marjorie laughed like Hades. She thought I was joking. I told her it was the truth.

"Jokes are often true," she said.

"So is tragedy."

"Goodness."

We talked for three more hours.

We talked about Kafka and Samuel Beckett. We talked about Karl Marx and Charles Darwin. We talked about abstract surrealism and cosmology. We talked about Eternalism and Nihilism. And we ended our conversation at quarter to three in the afternoon. And although many of our memories were fabricated and our stories appropriated from other sources, we'd never felt more vital or optimistic about our futures. But then we had to remind ourselves that fantasies can sometimes make you feel that way.

As I hung up the phone, I sighed. I think because I was tired. But it also could have been because I hadn't yet come to terms with my own bitterness. Bored, I looked out the window. A parade passed by. One of those parades where a quarter of the kids in the marching bands had forgotten their instruments and the clowns were all three drinks ahead of the mayor and two old Marines were riding in wheel chairs pushed by two old Daughters of the American Revolution and the floats resembled dioramas constructed by preschoolers and the spectators fell asleep and the Grand Marshall ordered sushi from his cell phone.

Suddenly there was a heavy, gloomy feeling in the air and I didn't quite feel at home or relaxed.

I felt like I was on the edge of something. Reality, maybe. Or maybe it was that I on the verge of something. A panic attack, perhaps. Hands numb, arms tingling, heart racing. I tried to do some deep-breathing exercises, thinking that might help to regain my equilibrium, but it only made me light headed and sleepy. So I took another shot of bourbon and laid down, fell asleep, had the usual slipstream dream. Or was it Dadaist? It was hard to tell; the images in this dream were filled with stylistic excess and looked like it was directed by an avant-garde poseur. Whatever it was, it was very post-apocalyptic. We'd been through some sort of disaster and the world was in ruins. By we, I mean us. Nobody knew for sure what had happened. There were speculations, of course. Nuclear war, plague, natural disaster. Some scientist from Coeur d'Alene, Idaho went on short wave radio claiming it was all carefully orchestrated and most likely a collaborative effort between the Bilderberg Group and the John Birch Society. The fact is, we'd simply been annihilated by something, some force beyond our human imaginations. Millions of people just spontaneously combusted. Others, like me, wandered aimlessly across the wasteland, trying to survive by any means possible.

Representatives from all of the Abrahamic religions met at an IHOP in

Oklahoma City to discuss what to do next. For some reason IHOPs were spared. The only thing anybody could agree on was that the omelets tasted like they were frozen and microwaved. At one point the Kabbalist turned to the Christian Martyr and said, "Do we have a generator and batteries?"

That's when I woke up.

I turned on the TV. There was a local public affairs show playing; a squat, fanatical little man was interviewing a stocky, arrogant woman.

Squat, Fanatical Little Man: "So God is a self-caused being."

Stocky Arrogant Woman: "Of course."

Squat, Fanatical Little Man: "But he didn't have parents."

Stocky, Arrogant Woman: "You're missing the point. God isn't under any obligation to reveal anything to us. Any of His works. He reveals what He wants to. On His own terms, in His own way. You can't get inside His head like that. You can't define God in human terms. He's like so far beyond our ability to conceptualize anything about Him. He's freakin' God, man!"

Squat, Fanatical Little Man: "But what kind of explanation is that? 'He's freakin' God?' What the hell does that mean? That doesn't mean *anything* to me. It just reinforces my belief that you really don't what the hell you're talking about!"

I turned off the TV, walked to the grocery store, bought a Swanson Hungry Man Turkey Dinner and a pecan pie.

On the way back I began to wonder if I'd be able to sustain this cool air of detachment I'd affected over the years. Because there seemed to be a hell of a lot of time left. And I laughed at myself as I unlocked the door to my apartment.

differences of view

The Mexican men at the Laundromat are smiling at each other and cracking jokes. There are a lot of references to someone or something being "estúpido loco."

The owner of the Laundromat, a heavy-set Asian man, leans against one of the folding tables and points a remote control device at a 13-inch black and white television set attached to a cheap ceiling mount.

After several minutes of watching a TV pastor dressed in combat fatigues calling people to Jesus Christ through the good news of the Gospel, he decides to change the channel and settle his tired eyes on *Showtime at the Apollo*.

A tiny Mexican man, in his best English, says to the owner, "Spanish channel?"

The owner laughs and in his best English says, "You think I got cable?"

The Mexican man laughs, as do all the other men sitting near the TV.

So *Showtime at the Apollo* it is, even though nobody watches it.

They're more interested in watching the spin cycle.

The ratings are through the roof.

If only network executives were there.

But network executives don't do coin-op Laundromats.

They barely do coins.

she's very tolerant of her behavioral problems

This story is not about you, so relax. It's about some other exceptionally naked nymphet who touched me in that nerve area like a Japanese Samurai, driving me to the point of exhaustion - who drank to dull the pain of a messy breakup and ended up paying her dues in one of those "intensive medical rehabilitation facilities" - who had a lot of anarchy in her and didn't conform to the expectations of what others held and always went her own way - who once told me I was a walking sore and never entirely outgrew my pubescent fascination with gimmicks - who was always looking at you with her eyes telling a story of her own triumph and tragedy and quarreling with anyone who wasn't moved by her misery - whose mercurial flickers of emotion and lacerating self-exposure often made me feel like I'd overdosed on jimson weed - who took all her sexual advice from Bill Clinton and only stayed in her last relationship because she was "fucked-up" and "addicted to it" - who played on other people's weaknesses and whose only challenges were the ones she imposed on herself - who had an understanding of suffering and was usually awake until 3 a.m. devising her next romantic coup.

So relax, this story is not about you.

And even if it was, you'd never recognize yourself, because there are too many others out there just like you. And I have only the gods to blame for that.

essence

There was a Disney movie on; something with Dean Jones or Kurt Russell or Fred MacMurray. I was on my second bottle of wine. I was painting. Didn't know exactly what I was painting, but brush was definitely touching canvas every now and then. I started out painting a still life, but it ended up looking more like a still born, so I painted over it, stood back, eyeing the colors. What colors there were. It looked like a puddle of vomit. I decided the hell with it. I was tired of trying to be a creator of emotions. Didn't have the patience or the talent.

So I walked outside with my bottle of wine and stared at the moon, thinking, *Jesus, feels like November out here*, even though it was April.

I looked at my watch. It was eight forty-five. I was tired, had a headache and a canker soar. I thought about my Mom's final words on her deathbed: "I did what was needed and didn't wait for anyone else to do it."

Somebody in the next yard was saying, "I know it sounds cornball, but we have to be OK with us inside first." Someone else said: "I know that. But how do I get to that point, is my problem." Someone else said: "It starts with self. 'To be or not to be'. Shakespeare. Think about it. And be, be you! Read Dr. Phil's *Self Matters*."

Then the voices trailed off. I think they went down by the riverside to smoke some pot and improve their personalities.

I would have liked to have gone with them but I really wasn't in the mood. That damn painting was still on my mind. Why couldn't I learn?

A ladybug suddenly landed on my right shoulder. I was about to blow her away but figured this was where she was meant to be right now, crawling down my arm, navigating her way through my arm hair. Why disrupt the natural order of things?

It started to sprinkle. I looked at the sky. It was smooth and black, but I could tell it was doing the slow burn. I felt a breeze on the nape of my neck and rain droplets on the crown of my head.

Meanwhile the ladybug had traveled toward my hand. Her trek had thus far been quite uneventful, but she suddenly appeared to be disorientated. Flustered. She spread her wings and flew away into the silky night, through the drops of rain.

I went inside to reevaluate my painting.

wait like kafka

I go to the movies on an empty stomach and on the way back, stop off at Dunkin' Donuts, inhale a half dozen doughnuts, then pull into a dingy little bar called Dipso's Delight, order a Seven and Seven, munch on stale peanuts, watch the Friday night fights, get into a philosophical discussion with a guy named Ned who admits to not knowing what the hell he's talking about half the time.

"It's like wandering around in some kinda daze," he says. "A fog, a mild nightmare, the kind that gets your heart racin', raises your blood pressure 20, 30 points. That's what my life has become…and they wonder why I stay the hell away from people."

Ned is a city employee, works in the information booth for the transit system, dispensing bus passes and educating the public at large on matters of public transportation. He's divorced, has two kids he sees every other weekend, and has a weakness for Tennessee white whiskey, unfiltered cigarettes and chili cheese dogs.

He wants to know if I have a girl.

"She thinks I'm a glass half-empty guy and this disturbs her," I say.

Ned smiles, shakes his head, lights another butt. "Like their moods are some kinda picnic," he says. "Listen, I been away from the triangle for quite some time now, and I'm not gonna lie to ya, I do occasionally get a little nostalgic for it. But I'm getting to the age where I just don't wanna hafta work for it like I usta. My days of hoop-jumping are over. Can't hang with the ladies like I usta. And I'm damn sure too tired to fake it."

He laughs, scratches his beard, takes a toothpick from a shot glass on the bar, and begins picking his teeth. "My advice to you," he says. "Is tell'er she needs to take the good with the bad. If she can't do that, she needs to become a nun, a lesbian or celibate. Tell'er that. She knows which side her bread's buttered on."

I finish my drink; thank him for the conversation, drive home, taking all the side roads.

When I get back to the apartment, my girl is lounging on the couch under a blanket sipping from a water glass filled to the brim with white zinfandel, watching some movie on HBO starring Pamela Anderson.

"Have fun?" she says with an edge.

"Look," I say. "You're just going to have to take the good with the bad. If you can't do that, you're going to have to become a nun, a lesbian or celibate. You know which side your bread's buttered on."

"You make a better door than a window," she says, then tells me I'm obstructing her view of the television.

I go to the bedroom, slam the door, sit down at the typewriter, type:

```
Nobody can make me feel guilty. Guilt is a man-
made emotion. It does not even exist!
```

There's a knock at the door.

"You alright?" she says.

"I'm busy! In the throes of creativity!"

She apologizes, her footsteps fade away.

I type:

```
I used to be afraid of being pussywhipped when I
was a younger man. Now I'm just afraid of being
alone.
```

I turn out the lights, fall asleep, dream the colors of newsprint and wait like Kafka.

fundamental human principles

Last weekend I went to one of those open mike nights where you get up and read your poetry in front of a bunch of espresso drinkers.

I read a piece about a cheerful but clueless ex-girlfriend whose favorite phrase was "to be continued, the saga continues."

As I read, my voice shook. I couldn't wait to finish. It was a pretty hostile poem, I guess. It was probably my revenge poem. I wrote about how she would always use her Cute Girl Voice to get me to do things and leave neurotic messages on my voicemail at three o'clock in the morning like, "I don't know why you're not answering your phone but I'm just gonna be standing out here on the curb in front of your building so when you get this message you'll know where to find me."

When I got off the stage, I was dumbfounded to find my clueless but cheerful ex-girlfriend leaning against a wall.

"Well," she said, lighting an herbal cigarette. "That was an interesting spin on our history."

I had a million lame excuses jogging through my mind but I didn't want to appear too defensive, given the gravity of her smirk, so I simply muttered something inaudible, hung my head in embarrassment and prayed that I'd get out of there with my balls intact.

"You have serious fucking anger management issues," she said.

I shrugged.

"Next thing you know you're gonna tell me 'it's only a fucken poem.'. I'm 'onna show you a poem."

Then, walking to the front of the room, she stood in front of the mike, cocky as shit.

"I call this one 'Who the Fuck is Moises Zurawski, Anyway?'. 'His eyes so deeply dark, dark like coal. He looks at you, he's very proud, he never bends his eyes. Every child thinks of death from time to time, I think that's quite natural, but I should say he thinks about death much more than others, just because he feels different and weaker than other people. People want to touch him, to look at him, to observe him. In the background of his self-portrait he draws a shadow and that's the shadow of the devil. He's drinking. When he runs out of wine, he begins to consume turpentine. Candles are lit. A Bach fugue plays on the phonograph. I watch in awe as he produces a knife and attacks the portrait. With rare violence he cuts the paper and says, I hate you, I hate you, I hate you! And then he takes a brush, red paint, and paints blood around the scars.'"

The audience gave her a standing ovation. I don't know why. I didn't think it was that great. I certainly didn't think it deserved a standing ovation.

As she brushed passed me she said, "Touché, motherfucker," and headed for the exit.

Stupidly, I followed her.

"Why'd you use my name?" I said.

She blew a cloud of smoke into the chill night. "Nobody knows who you are."

"I didn't use your name."

"Hunh," she said.

There was so much adrenalin pumping through me I didn't know what the hell to say. That was the way it always was with us. I think that was why we broke up.

"Do you know what the secret to being a hero is?" she said.

"What's that?"

"Reluctance. And being able to act in an appropriately violent manner."

I shook my head. "I still don't understand a damn thing you say."

"Hey, I'm the product of seven different foster homes," she said. "Me and Norma Jean."

"Who?"

"Marilyn Monroe."

It started to drizzle.

She offered her hand, I shook it. "Keep writing," she said.

"You too," I said.

She hailed a cab, got in, told the driver to take her to the airport.

"Where you going?" I said.

"Hawaii."

"How come?"

"Leave me alone," she said. "I'm tired of your ass."

And she drove off.

Like an idiot I stood there, soaking wet, thinking, *these are just fundamental human principles.*

Luckily I held my tongue.

Like I had a choice.

it's about the fable you want to write about your own life

New Year's Day morning. Turn on the TV. Notoriously melodramatic holiday fare about a deathly dull financier accused of engaging in a series of unlawful security transactions attempting to negotiate a deal with an angel for his immortal soul.

"What if I plead guilty to lesser securities and reporting violations?" said the financier.

"God doesn't do plea bargains."

"What if I became born-again?"

"Puhlease."

"I could launch a foundation whose mission would be to support education and medical research!"

"God has a much better plan for you."

"What's that?"

"You will live in subsidized housing on 105th Street in Cleveland, Ohio's Glenville neighborhood on an income below Federal poverty guidelines for the rest of your natural life. And when you die you will be banished to Hell for all eternity."

"*Christ*! Is that the best He can do?"

Suddenly the financier was turned into a pillar of salt.

The angel smiled. "No, actually, *that's* the best He can do."

Turn off the TV. Light a Dominican hand-made cigar. Try to think of something intellectually challenging. Can't. Pick up a cheap paperback novel I purchased the night before at the drug store titled, "Pity is a Step Away from Abuse," and re-read the introduction:

"He looked like dissipated Eurotrash in his Alfani wool coat, headband, and gigantic sunglasses. He had a masculine quality but there was also an androgynous and criminal element going on there. Something that said, 'Transgression is exciting to me.'"

Flip to Chapter 1.

"He woke up at two minutes past three. He'd had a very difficult year. It began last February when his soon-to-be ex-girlfriend broke into his apartment and smashed his steel string guitar (autographed by Esteban) and sliced into the heads of his collection of talking drums with a Ginsu knife for cheating on her with a not-so-discreet-and-exclusive escort who turned out to be her roommate's sister."

Who the hell writes this shit? Close the book. Fall asleep.

Have that reoccurring dream where I'm hauled in front of some ambiguous tribunal for allegedly "frittering away the last twenty years of my life."

The Judge, who's on his third Dirty Martini, dressed in a tuxedo with some medals on it, brings down the gavel. "You stand accused of allowing your life to go down the drain, of not working hard enough, not being ambitious enough, vibrant enough, alive enough."

"Really?"

"Also of deluding yourself, being too quiet, too reserved, too intense, angry, selfish, self-indulgent, complicated, confused, of luring unsuspecting women into the sack with promises of this, that, and the other thing; blah blah blah, blah blah blah… How do you plead?"

"It takes two to tango, baby."

"Son, you are in flagrant contempt of court!"

"I'm sorry, Your Honor, but there are a million different ways to live your life. I can't help it if you don't understand or appreciate my idiosyncrasies."

"That's not the point. You had promise. Talent. People had expectations of you. They believed in you. Do you realize how many people you've disappointed with your complacency? Your nonchalance? Your passivity?"

"Are they really disappointed in me? Or in themselves?"

Judge leans forward. Hiccups. "Son…" Takes a sip of his Martini. "Haven't you ever had any dreams and aspirations?"

"Just to live a simple, contented life, Your Honor."

"Well, son, do you believe in God?"

"I'm considering it."

Judge sighs. "Well, I have no other choice but to sentence you to…"

Just then the angel from the movie I was watching earlier materializes. Lying on the judge's bench. "I'll take it from here, Your Honor."

I snap awake. In a warm sweat. Sigh. Light another cigar. Watch another New Year yawn. Resolve not to give a damn about becoming a man of legend and folklore.

weight and inertia and all that mumbo jumbo

My life has always been like an advanced geometry problem; a perfect balance of applied physics and my extreme human ability. Always figuring out my angle of approach versus the speed. It works out great although it's really hard on the body. So much exposure there, but seems so comfortable standing there. Even as a boy, I demonstrated a spirit of fearlessness and an appetite for danger and was able to absorb and smooth out the shocks of my life. It was just a matter of breaking through that fear barrier and seeing how much pressure it took to break me; turns out I don't break, I just bend. Yeah, I made it down in one piece and kept it together. I'm still here.

crises of faith

prologue

It's one of those days when I wake up at 6 in the morning, look in the mirror and say, "Lord, help me" before I realize it's Sunday and don't even have to go to work. So I stare at my unshaven face and think, *Well, Christ, since I hate shaving so much, I ought to just grow a damn beard,* but I reconsider once I see all those tiny gray hairs jutting out like monkey grass from my flabby, antiquated jaw.

After taking a foaming vanilla honey bath and jerking off to the Slovakian hermaphrodite next door, (because sometimes I just can't help myself), I flop back into bed like a heart-broken penguin unable to find its mate after traveling three months across a frozen landscape, and worry that I might be plateauing. Not only because I'm jerking off to Slovakian hermaphrodites, but because in between sips of a Jägerbomb the other night at a club I only hang out at when I'm rolling like that, I actually admitted to a friend with occasional benefits that I often feel like I'm "a ghostly form swaying beneath the gray twilight."

That I even uttered such an emotionally-disturbed-fourteen-year-old girl-writing-in-her-diary phrase while I was stone-cold sober is worrisome enough. That I said it while wearing a cock ring around my tongue just proves what a saggy-breasted, toe-sucking communist plebian I really am.

Leave it to my friend with the chip on her shoulder the size of Camille Paglia's ass to put it all in perspective for me, though: "Does it not seem rather a waste of valuable energy to invent so many falsehoods?"

And she's absolutely right.

Which reminds me of the time she had to take a shame shower immediately after I anally abused her.

So much for falsehoods.

Meanwhile, back at the ranch...

As I enter a less-than-ducky REM sleep, (face-down in a pillow that has all the support of a twenty year old bed-sheet), I have that ridiculous reoccurring dream of being baptized in a puddle of Zima by a ninety year old defrocked priest with goiters and breath that smells like the back room of a gay bar in Budapest. On the Pest side, of course.

Mercifully, I'm awakened by the bone-splintering shrieks of the kid next door whose mother is probably breaking down the tragedies of life to him by making him watch a slide show of my love life on his Fisher-Price View-Master.

"Now, you see, Timmy, this is what happens to a man once he has achieved the emotional maturity of a parasitic protozoa."

After staring at the water stain on the ceiling that looks like an abstract painting by an autistic monkey, I go a few rounds with my psyche until my psyche delivers a left that puts me down and in deep trouble. However I manage to stay on my feet despite the barrage of right uppercuts to my cerebrum. But I land a monster right cross and a furious flurry of one-two combinations and counterpunches and my psyche begins to show the effects of my hard punching. After two more grueling rounds, I decide to concede defeat and resign myself to my congenital sadness rather than risk developing dementia from all those blows to the mind. Because the tragedy of my truth as I know it to be or not to be usually causes me to detach and emotionally escape by ingesting copious amounts of psychotropic substances, and I'm getting way too old for those short, familiar trips. So keeping my eyes off the clock, I drift off to sleep again, hoping that my memory foam pillow that I suddenly remember is underneath my bed will allow me to forget about the last half hour of my life.

epilogue

I grew up thinking the hero suffers, travels a path of self-discovery, learns a few lessons, finds some redemption and gets the girl.

However I've come to a realization. I've realized that the very same atoms that are in you and me are the same atoms that are in all the rest of the universe and those atoms came from the middle of one star. So that's really us up there. Sort of puts a whole new perspective on this ego thing. What psychologists refer to as our ego. How we spend our whole lives trying to convince ourselves that we're something. That we alone have this unique and transcendent value above all other creatures. Our souls were created from nothing by God and we've been blessed with the spark of divine nature, which guarantees us, alone, among all creatures, a chance for an endless life. When in reality we just might be a big fat zero. But who the hell wants to accept that? That's why we have an ego, to remind ourselves that we're not nothing.

But I kind of like the idea that we're nothing. It comforts me. Takes the pressure off of me to be too successful.

her sacred atonal life

Mayzie was on stage at a slam competition reading from Isaiah 47.

"'And thou saidist, I shall be a lady for ever: so that thou dist not lay these things to thy heart, neither didst remember the latter end of it.'"

Just then, a decrepit, tipsy middle-aged man in a cheap suit stood up on his chair, and hollered hoarsely, "'Wrath is cruel, and the anger is outrageous; but who is able to stand before envy?'"

Mayzie shielded her eyes from the lights with her hand to get a clearer vision of the heckler.

"Daddy?" she said.

"'Open rebuke is better than secret love,'" said the man.

"Daddy?!"

The man got off his chair, and walked toward the stage holding a mentholated cigarette between his fingers. "'A continual dropping in a very rainy day and a contentious woman are alike.'"

As the man climbed onto the stage, he wobbled momentarily, and then lost his balance, falling pathetically in front of his startled daughter, who squatted to his aid.

"Daddy, are you alright?"

"It never ceases to amaze me," the man said, pausing to blow a smoky sigh out of the corner of his mouth. "'Hell and destruction are never full; so the eyes of man are never satisfied'" He began sobbing quietly. "She was always there, your mother…she was very clever…give her a mirror and she turned it into a drama…it was as if she were irreplaceable…there was this incredible reaction between her and her clothes…a personality hidden somewhere in her face…"

"Daddy, please don't."

"Is this how it's going to be, Mayzie? Is this what it's come to? Settling for…Is this it?"

"What are you talking about?"

"You've always been so strong...everybody, all your teachers said, Mayzie's such a brilliant student, she's so..." He trailed off, and then mumbled, "Magna cum laude."

"Valedictorian."

"Straight A's, the honor roll, 1500 on your SAT's, scholarships to..."

"I did it all for you," Mayzie said.

"1955 I was living in Boston, off of Commonwealth Avenue, going to B.U. when I got the call from my father...a flood had destroyed the store...he needed my help...I told him I couldn't come home then, I was right in the middle of finals...he said, 'Screw your finals.' I told him if I don't take my finals, I don't graduate...and he hung up on me...I tried to call him back; it just kept ringing...even my mother wouldn't talk to me..."

"I know the story."

"So I took the first bus home..."

"And you did it for him."

He paused. There was an underlying bitterness in his tone. "God*dammit*, I don't have the energy to build you back up again."

"Excuse me?"

"You were such a..."

"I was such a what? I was so lonely and you always denied me my feelings."

"Ohh crap!"

Mayzie was on the verge of tears. "You never allowed me to be unhappy!"

"Because I had enough unhappiness for the whole goddamn family!"

Neither one had the energy to say anything. Mayzie wept. Her father continued his wall-eyed stare. He began to break down, but tried to suppress his tears. "What happened to you is *I* happened to you...I knew what you were going through… I knew your pain because it was *my* pain… and I allowed you to be unhappy, I gave you every opportunity to be as miserable as you wanted to be." Then he screamed. "YOU WERE MY LIFE WHEN MY LIFE FAILED!"

The stunned audience sat in confused silence for several moments. Then a single lonely pair of hands began to clap, followed shortly by another lonely pair of hands, then another and another.

Soon the entire audience was on their feet, cheering, whistling, whooping and hollering.

Mayzie took home first prize that night and was awarded fifty dollars for her slam, even though it wasn't a slam at all.

The following week, Mayzie brought her mother with her to another open-mike night competition.

As she stepped to the mike, she looked into the audience, caught her mother's eyes and said, "'Who can find a virtuous woman? For her price is far above pearls.'"

full of pretenses

Went to the library. Asked the sort-of sexy librarian for a book written by a guy who thought he had a handle on his emotions but had come undone following an Up with People performance in Montpelier, Vermont.

The librarian pecked a few keys on her keyboard, squinting at the monitor for what seemed like twenty-seven point eight seconds.

"Yes, sir, we do have that title. It's called *Confused, Anxious, and Angry: One Man's Downward Spiral into an Anonymous Abyss.*" Suddenly, her eyes narrowed, and she scrunched-up her face. "Ooooh. That sounds awfully depressing."

From that point on she avoided eye-contact with me. "Adult nonfiction," she said sternly, not offering to help me locate it.

I walked through the maze of shelves.

By the time I found the call number and the book, I needed a nap.

The book was old and well-worn; it had last been checked out eighteen years ago, and before that, only a handful of times. Pages were loose, the spine was damaged, but somehow, after all these years, the jacket had survived. Scattered throughout the book's margins were handwritten comments like: "Bite me," or "I like this," or "Interesting," or "Bullshit horseshit," or "Be careful. Gladys has Chlamydia." Entire passages were either highlighted with a yellow highlighter or underlined with a fat, messy ballpoint pen. I thought it must be a pretty worthwhile book if people actually took the time to underline and highlight it.

I flipped to the back of the book, looked at the author's picture (for a guy who'd just experienced a downward spiral into an anonymous abyss, he looked relatively happy) and read his bio:

"Jasper E. Wiggins was born in Buddha, Indiana and educated at North American University, where he received a legal, accredited law degree in twenty-seven days. As a kid he was always goofing around and falling off his bike and playing around with his mother's funny hats and things like that. He now lives in Monkey's Eyebrow, Arizona, where he says he's sometimes confused about his future and identity. In his spare time, he plays the banjo while watching the *Lawrence Welk Show* and makes hemp jewelry."

I opened the book to page 421 and focused my eyes on the fourth paragraph.

"He believed in his Lord, his God, though they were not on very intimate terms. He went to church, but mostly because he felt guilty for not going. The women in his life didn't think he had much get-up-and-go, but they liked his sense of humor and the sadness in his heart, which they found absolutely fascinating and made them curious. His parents, who never had the courage of discovery, abandoned him at the age of five, gave him up for adoption, and hid from their destiny, their own tribunal. (It's all symbolic)."

I stopped reading at that point, closed the book, and headed for the check-out counter.

the likeness is quite exact

I tip my hat to the dwarf with the beautiful Italian shoes.

He's just quit smoking. Yesterday. He's been to the doc, donated some tissue samples, won't tell me why, though, just that "they've found some abnormalities."

I look for a hook in the conversation, but can't find one.

Or rather he doesn't want me to find one.

He doesn't smile. He's too self-conscious. "Five cracked teeth," says the dwarf. "And all I got left are smirks for all the ladies."

His jaw is all stubbly; it keeps the world at large at bay.

I go through my pockets, try to find my watch, but it's not there.

I look at the big clock on top of the town hall.

The hands are missing.

The dwarf isn't surprised. "Been that way for years," he says. "Town council keeps saying, 'Oh, there's no money.' But we all know where the money's really going."

"Where is it going?"

He points toward a prostitute.

I'm just about to ask him to explain that when out comes the Mayor, skipping rope.

He's much taller than I imagined. He's also incredibly well coordinated. I'd always admired his sense of something or other. He stops skipping rope, glad-hands the dwarf, asks him for a smoke.

"Sorry, Mister Mayor, I quit yesterday."

The Mayor seems angry. "What the hell did you go and do a thing like that for?" he says.

The dwarf shrugs. "Just felt like it."

The Mayor sizes me up. "How 'bout you, son?"

"No, sir," I say.

"Don't tell me you quit, too?"

"No, sir, I never started."

"Oh, one of *those*," the Mayor says, eyeing the prostitute. "Well, boys, really love to stick around and chat, but got places to go, people to see, you know how it is."

The Mayor pats me on the shoulder, pats the dwarf on the head, walks over to the prostitute and bums a cigarette from her.

They stand facing one another, laughing, joking, flirting.

I overhear him asking her if she voted for him in the last election.

She's all coy and her cheeks are rosy. "I don't vote," says the prostitute.

"You don't? How come?"

"I don't know…just doesn't seem like it matters *who's* in office."

The Mayor pauses in thoughtful repose. "Hmm. Well. Why don't I buy you a cup of coffee and explain to you exactly why it *does* matter?"

"OK."

They disappear into Bert's Neighborhood Grille.

"What I tell ya?" cracks the dwarf, offering me a slug from a flask.

"No thanks," I say.

"Dude, it's Jack Daniels."

"Don't touch the stuff."

"Sinatra drank J.D. Two fingers, the rest water. He also liked his Martinis chilled and dry with an olive."

"I'm a Lou Reed guy," I say.

The dwarf nods. "When he was with Velvet Underground."

"Even after."

The dwarf takes a hit from the flask, shrugs.

The wind picks up.

The dwarf begins wobbling back and forth.

"Hooo, feel a little woozy," he says, and falls to the ground.

"You alright?" I say.

"Just need to rest for a quick minute. I'll be alright." And he falls asleep.

As I head for Bert's Neighborhood Grille for some hot coffee and scrambled eggs, I hear the dwarf mumbling in his sleep.

"No moral payoff…madness and surrealism…short-circuiting my analytical capacities…Good luck to you and give'em hell…I am not in love, just buzzing on dopamine…"

I sit down at the counter, order my breakfast and for the first time that day, resolve to keep my eyes off the clock.

a distillation of the human experience

I've ignored some really important life lessons:

1. Embracing your uniqueness at the risk of losing family/friends.
2. One person can make a difference.
3. Inevitable loss of innocence.
4. The necessity of sacrifice.
5. Growth through pain and rebirth.
6. The value of having a dream.
7. The redemptive power of art, beauty, or nature.
8. Resisting bullies.
9. Seeing both sides of the story.

Ignored them because I was more concerned with testing others' will power and self-control and feeling spiritually dangerous than with going through the process of figuring out if one person can have an effect on history.

So I left town.

I was torn between destiny and true love in a universe parallel to ours where the mysteries of the past were revealed, and a new legacy was born.

There were jobs every now and then. Knife thrower's assistant, coffin maker, potato chip inspector, golf ball diver.

But enough was enough.

Next came my brandy-drinking, Newport-smoking, trench coat and black jeans period where I obsessed over the mutability of the universe and engaged in small, bitter games in lieu of tackling some of the really tough existential questions like:

What, truly, brought me to the brink of blasphemy?

What demons made me so emotionally uncandid, and are they still chasing me?

Was that self-harming emo beauty with the laissez-faire approach to sex really my last chance at love?

Then I got, like, kind of empty.

Became detached and sullen.

Grew my hair below my shoulders.

Slept on a stiff cardboard box and tattered foam covered with thin blankets on a concrete slab under an overpass, subsisting on desperation and Mussolini's boyhood diet of vegetable soup and unleavened bread

I'd wake each morning with the disquieting feeling that I was in constant jeopardy; like one of those no-name characters in a Spaghetti Western. Some felt it was because I was saying goodbye to my innocent personae; while others preferred to reserve judgment until I sobered up from my pipedreams.

The truth is I was a mass of neurotic doubts and it was becoming more difficult for me to maintain a lot of the continuity that came before me, so I did what any red-blooded, passive-aggressive ne'er-do-well would have done under such a fucked-up situation. I got drunk. Every night for six months. So drunk, that one night I apparently stumbled into one of those all-night "houses of worship" and allegedly converted my ass to something. God knows what, but the following morning, after I crawled out of an old, rusty cast iron bathtub, I was told by this weird, rough-looking dude who called himself "The Right Mufti" that I was now a member of the People Who Love People Church and, as he raised a pocket-sized, vinyl-bound book into the air, he shouted, "As the Greatest Book says, 'Knock at thy door and ye shall be taken in!'"

That's when thee's door was busted down by a couple of DEA agents brandishing submachine guns, who arrested the "Right Mufti" on charges of the production and distribution of methamphetamines and ephedrines.

Which is when I closed thou's door forever on binge-drinking and began dedicating my life to working out that tight little problem of learning how to reinvent myself without compromising my newfound moral principles.

And now that I've aged into a damaged, angry, lovable hustler hero, struggling to keep my rage in check and attempting to control my temper and my volatile, unstable impulses so I can face the final initiation into adulthood by sifting through the complexities and sadness of emotional truth, I find that my run-on sentences do the 40-yard dash in 4.38 seconds and I'm not so quick to tumble into bed with profoundly lonely chicks with long hair, tight clothes, fake nails, heaving, well-implanted breasts.

It's funny.

I used to think I was the only one with banal frustrations, the only one shouldering terrifying responsibilities and overwhelmed with disillusionment and doubt, the only one holding onto adolescent sarcasm and tempted by hubris and despair.

But clearly I'm not.

I'm just another angsty and brooding protagonist who is just this side of crazy and has unusually little love life and meddles in things Man was not meant to know, hoping I can at least learn not to ignore the Most Important Life Lesson of all:

10. There is no glory in being another study of so many things disintegrating.

who's sid vicious?

And so our record deal disintegrated right before our eyes and we went back to playing high school proms and bars with names like The Imp's Tavern and The Vulgar Dog.

It didn't dawn on us until we were uncomfortably well into our thirties that we were quickly approaching obsolescence.

Denny, the drummer, came to us after a particularly grueling Battle of the Bands contest and announced his retirement from the band.

"I'm gettin' carpal tunnel, man," he said, shaking his head and walking away without looking at any of us.

There would be no more tributes to the Sex Pistols or the Dead Kennedys, no more all-nighters, no more living five to a six-hundred square foot studio apartment with every imaginable rodent and insect occupying our living space, no more knocks on the door in the middle of the night from the LAPD following up on reports of loud music and fights in the parking lot, no more getting stiffed by bar owners, no more getting stiff for girls who were older than sixteen, (we swear to God), no more of those alleged sixteen year old girl's fathers threatening to blow our heads off, no more bloody noses, no more accidental overdoses, no more girlfriends named Feather and Sparkle.

The soggy, foggy dream was over.

And in spite of the fact that we had no discernible job skills whatsoever, we all got gigs with the U.S. Postal Service as temporary rural route carriers, and even though it bores the hell out of us, we've found that our pillows are a little softer at night and the women we date now have no idea who Sid Vicious was.

They just like the steady income.

more prophetic than any of us can imagine

Michael: You there?

Gracie: Yep.

Michael: So how are you?

Gracie: Uhmm… I don't know.

Michael: What's going on?

Gracie: Can you hold on a minute?

Michael: Yeah.

(pause. Gracie gets back on the phone)

Gracie: OK, I'm back.

Michael: So whucha thinking?

Gracie: I'm thinking I don't like this Merlot.

Michael: Ohh.

Gracie: I like that cheap Merlot. The five dollar and forty-nine cent bottle. You know the one I'm talking about?

Michael: I think so.

Gracie: (sigh) Oh well… (sound of her taking a sip) I have a lot of disquiet going on in my life at the moment. I'm just trying to remain calm.

Michael: I know disquiet.

Gracie: I'm reading this book that says all of us has a champion that lives deep down inside of us. Do you believe that?

Michael: I guess…somewhat.

Gracie: I don't know what they mean by it but it sounds like a good thing to put in a book.

Michael: Uh heh.

(pause)

Gracie: Somebody told me the other day I'm complex.

Michael: Really?

Gracie: That I have just sub layers and sub layers to my personality. I don't even know what anybody means anymore…like the other day a friend of mine says, "I'm the kind of person that needs someone I can always beat up on." I was like, whaa? I've known this person for like twelve years. I never would've thought they would've come out with something like that in a million years. This person's very quiet, soft-spoken, polite. Totally not the bullying type. I was like, whoa, wait a minute, I really don't know this person at all. I think inevitably whenever you're dealing with people you want to create the strongest possible alliance humanly possible…(reconsiders) Or not.

Michael: Yeah.

(pause)

Gracie: I hope I'm not wasting your time?

Michael: No ma'am.

Gracie: Do you think I'm afraid to fully confront the adult world and that I'm narcissistic and self-absorbed and standoffish and shut off emotionally and that I spend too much time alone?

Michael: Wow, those are some questions.

(slight pause)

Gracie: Would you like to take a stab at answering any of them?

Michael: Yeah I think you're all of those things.

Gracie: Me too. Listen to this. (reading from a notebook) "This morning I wake with a profound sense of excitement and fear. Excitement because

I'm near you. Fear because I lose my balance and have trouble expressing my feelings."

Michael: (slight pause) Hmmm.

Gracie: "Everything about my life is about getting out there and giving back. It's easy to get lost in what I'm doing. My first instinct is always good."

Michael: What are you reading from?

Gracie: My sister's diary. When she was 14.

Michael: Why do you have it?

Gracie: Finders keepers.

Michael: Don't you think you should give it back to her?

Gracie: Actually, I don't. She's taken more than her share from me over the years.

Michael: What has she taken from you?

Gracie: Let's see. She took my mood ring, my clodhoppers, my Sloppy Joe, my culottes, my micro miniskirt, my pea coat, my legwarmers, my leotards, my hemp bracelet, my best of *The Brady Bunch* and *Partridge Family* albums, my copy of *Franny and Zooey*. Watch. Hold on.

Michael: Wha?

Gracie: I'm gonna do a three way.

Michael: A what?

Gracie: Shhh…(puts Michael on hold. pause. she gets back on. sound of a number ringing) You there?

Michael: Who are you calling?

Gracie: Shh. Don't say anything.

Michael: Hunh?

Gracie: Shhhh!

Voice: (female) Hello?

Gracie: Hi, Patty, it's Gracie.

Patty: (somewhat indifferent) Grace, I'm on another call, I can't talk right now.

Gracie: Remember all that stuff you took from me?

Patty: (slight pause) What stuff?

Gracie: My mood ring, my clodhoppers, my best of the *Brady Bunch* and *Partridge Family* albums, my copy of *Franny and Zooey*? That stuff.

Patty: (pause; edgy) Okaay?

Gracie: I just want you to know I haven't forgotten about it.

Patty: (pause) So what's your point? You took reams of my poetry, my extremely *personal* poetry, made mimeograph copies of it and then proceeded to distribute them on Christmas Eve to all the parishioners at the conclusion of Midnight Mass. I don't call you up every time I'm drunk and depressed to remind you of that.

Gracie: I'm not drunk or depressed. I just want you to know I haven't forgotten about it.

Patty: Grace, make an appointment with a really good therapist and relieve yourself of all this childhood guilt and angst you seem so sure exists. You're a big girl, it's time to grow up, take control, and keep it moving.

Gracie: (whatever) OK.

Patty: G'bye.

Gracie: Uh heh. (click; to Michael) Tol'ja.

Michael: Wow

Gracie: Charming, isn't she? (reading) "People just don't notice me the way I notice them. I'm growing up in a blink of an eye. There has to come the moment where you look at yourself and look at everybody else in your life and think, 'Whether or not you're going to stay with me after what I'm about to say, is up to you, but I need to put myself first now. Not ignoring you. But it's me first. And whether or not you approve of my decisions, I can't let that concern me anymore.'" (pause) That's another one of her poems.

Michael: Interesting.

Gracie: Very interesting.

(blackout)

the radar was awash with hot reds and blues

Had a collage of ideas brainstorming inside of me. There was a high-pressure system moving up my spinal column. The heat-index in my genital area was a hundred plus, the winds were blowing north/northeasterly and gusting up to 70 miles an hour in the canals of my ears.

I had to take an antidepressant to calm the seas, otherwise the waves would have crashed over me and sent me plummeting to the depths of the abyss where oxygen is scarce and the sharks and the piranhas would detect my lifeblood and bleeding ulcer.

Then somebody threw me a life preserver (it was my analyst), but it was made of cement.

An old man in the sea hooked me on his sword fishing pole (using booze as bait) but when he pulled me onto his boat, he told me I was below the legal limit, removed the bottle from my mouth and returned me to my watery limbo.

Then an elderly mariner sailed passed me, shook his ancient head and pointed to the albatross around his neck. "I'm already way in over my head," he said.

I treaded water for months.

I caught Swimmer's ear listening to the sound of the ocean in a seashell.

I happened upon a double-amputee mermaid.

She said, "I'm looking for my fatal charm. I seem to have lost it. Can you help me find it?"

"I hear they're doing wonderful things with prosthetics these days," I said.

Disappointed, her torso swam away. (I never did have much of a rap with the ladies).

My lousy luck with women began in the womb. I'd roundhouse kick my mother like a martial artist. She'd fight back by punching her belly. "Don't you ever do that to me again!" she'd scream. The match lasted nine months. The judges scored it a draw. There was not a rematch.

Ironically, a parochial school of fish came to my aid. I told them I was Jewish. "That's alright," they mused. "We have very catholic tastes."

"It doesn't bother you that I don't believe in the Holy Trinity or Immaculate Conception?"

"Down here there's only one school of thought," the leader of the parish said. "Sink or swim."

the silence is best

A man, calling himself Peabody, calls up a radio talk show and tells the host he lives in a 23-room mansion, has three Rolls Royce's, a '69 Corvette, and is one of the loneliest people in the world.

"Come on, Peabody," the host says. "You have no friends?"

"I have one or two acquaintances I associate with on occasion."

"So, that's probably all you need. Why are you living alone in a 23-room mansion?"

"Because I want to," Peabody says, laughing.

"No wife? No girlfriend? I'm assuming you're not gay, which is a very dangerous thing to assume these days."

"I'm not gay. I just don't like people."

"You're a misanthrope."

"Well," says Peabody, pausing. "I guess you could say that."

"You don't need people."

Another pause. "Not especially, no."

"So what's the problem? You shouldn't be lonely."

Peabody chuckles. "Shouldn't be. But I am."

"Peabody, I find it difficult to believe that you cannot make friends."

"Oh I can make 'em. I just can't keep 'em."

"Why can't you keep them?"

"Because I don't always tell 'em what they wanna hear. If I don't like someone or somethin' about 'em, I tell 'em."

"Oh great," the host says. "You're one of these brutally honest guys -"

" That's me -"

" - who goes around hurting everybody's feelings."

"Well - the truth sometimes hurts, Jerry - doesn't it?"

"It does. But is telling the truth, at the expense of hurting another's feelings, worth the price of loneliness? My God, that was profound. Did you find that as profound as I did, Peabody?"

"I did."

"Hey, by the way. Why three Rolls Royce's? What is it about three Rolls Royce's?"

"I like 'em. I like to look at 'em."

"Why not a Pacer? Now there was a great car."

Peabody laughs.

"So, what do you do all day, Peabody, besides looking at your three Rolls Royce's?"

"I write, I draw, I paint. I talk to people on the phone."

"Don't get out much, do you?"

"Not anymore, Jerry, I err… have retreated into my own little cocoon here."

"No special lady friend?"

Pause. "Not at the present time."

"Afraid of the gold digger aspect?"

"Hell, I couldn't care less about that. I've given plenty of money away to women."

"Is that right? Ever been married?"

"No, sir."

"Oh well, you're in the clear, then. No alimony, no giving up half of what you own. May I ask how old a man you are, Peabody?"

"I'm fifty-seven."

"Ever fathered any children?"

"Not to my knowledge or recollection."

"A simple yes or no will do, Peabody. What are you, a radio talk show host?"

Peabody laughs.

"Peabody, be honest. Have you ever worked a day in your life?"

"Well, my father was a billionaire."

"A billionaire?"

"Yessir."

"OK, so let's recap for a moment. You had a billionaire father. You're fifty-seven years old, never been married, no children to your knowledge or recollection, you live alone in a 23-room mansion, you have three Rolls Royce's, a '69 Corvette, you sit home all day writing and drawing and painting and talking on the phone and you're one of the loneliest guys in the world."

"That about sums it up," Peabody says, chuckling.

"Well, hell, I'll buy that. What did your billionaire father do?"

"Can't really say. I think people are already beginning to get an idea of who I am and I'd rather not divulge any of that at this juncture."

"Well, Peabody? Can I tell you something, my friend? You fascinate me. I don't believe a word you say, but you fascinate me on so many different levels."

"I'll send you pictures."

"And how will I know they're not pictures of somebody else's 23-room mansion, three Rolls Royce's, and '69 Corvette. How will I know this?"

"Jerry, I guarantee, even you probably know who I am."

"Yes, but the real question is, Do I really care? Anyway, send me those pictures, Peabody, and stop being so lonely!"

"I'll try, Jerry."

"And go out and find yourself a nice girl, for cryin' out loud!"

"The operative word there is 'nice.'"

"There's no pleasing you, is there, Peabody?"

"It's very difficult."

"That's what I thought. Gotta go, my friend. Don't ever change."

"Love the show."

"I love it, as well. Off he goes. Let's hear it for Peabody, the lonely son of a billionaire. You buyin' it? Naaah, didn't think so." Bumper music drops in. "I still don't know what he's got against Pacers. Do you remember the Gremlin? How 'bout The Thing. Remember The Thing? That piece of crap Volkswagen put out in the 70s for about a week and a half? Yeah, I had one. It was yellow. Is yellow not the most hideous color for a car? Felt like the biggest schmuck. Now here was a car, if you were a guy and had the misfortune of driving around in this tin box, no respect! Right? Am I right? People on mopeds looked down their noses at you. Not only *that*. You did not get laid while driving this car - for however long you owned it - I don't care how good looking you were, I don't care how much money you had - this car was truly repellent to women, and you got bupkes! I, personally, remained celibate for three and a half years while owning this car. No respect! If you ever - *ever* see me in a car like this again, shoot me. You have my permission to end my life. Here's another thing: if you ever see me out in public wearing a white sleeveless tee shirt tucked into a bathing suit, black socks and sandals, shoot me. If you ever see me with a bad toupee, shoot me. If you ever see me with a comb over, shoot me. If you ever see my wife and I wearing matching outfits, shoot me. If you ever see me dying my hair back to its original color when I'm eighty, shoot me. If you ever see me alone in a 23-room mansion with three Rolls Royce's and a '69 Corvette, shoot me. Peabody, buddy, just kiddin', my man! For God's sakes, get a sense of humor. And a life. We'll be back. Sheesh, some people are so damn sensitive."

she jives by night

Boy: I love you…

Girl: I love you, too…I think…

Boy: How do you know?

Girl: 'Cuz i feel it…

I recalled a distant lover who was a little in, a little out, and a little more out, who would use a calculator to add up the sum total of her existence.

She was addicted to sugary cereals and had a very difficult upbringing, trusted very few people and needed to be coddled with a lot of psychoanalytical mumbo jumbo.

They all thought she was just a Stoli and blow debutante with a history of blowing a .07 into breathalyzers, possessing a get-out-now mentality, and thinking it was always time for payback.

But I didn't care; she could talk a living language and was always moving in on my brain and making my water a little hot.

One foggy Christmas Eve, we were drinking some clear malt liquor (it was all the priest had), in the backseat of my '66 Chevy Chevelle, when she suddenly said, "Look down my throat. What do you see?"

"There's a slight rosiness."

"It's hot and it's wet."

"Uh heh."

"Sound familiar?"

And then she put a maneuver down my spine that caused me to instantly ejaculate inside my boxer-briefs.

After I recovered, she looked at me through pinkish-white irises, and said, "You're a Sagittarius, aren't you?"

"Yes. Why?"

"Ya'll are always walkin' around with a shell between you and the rest of humanity. Always trying to be a daredevil with your own fate. God knows I love ya, though."

Her snaking tongue slithered across the edges of my teeth and she slid a finger under her panties and began caressing herself. "Mmmm. Did you know Cleopatra committed suicide by placing an asp to her bosom?"

I tried to shake my head, but it was wedged between the door and the backseat.

"Personally, I believe she would have gotten more bang for her buck had she allowed it to nibble on her clit a little bit. But perhaps that's just my unaccepted vulgarism talking."

Suddenly her eyes rolled back within her head and her body was twisting and bucking and twitching like she was experiencing the clonic phase of a grand mal seizure. I thought she was going to kick out the windows with her legs. I'd never seen a woman come so quickly or so intensely.

When her orgasmic tremors finally subsided a few minutes later, she looked at me and smiled.

"You certainly know how to put a woman in her universe," she said, and she drifted off to sleep.

I took one last pull from my malt beverage and reveled in the fact that there were no heroics, no gunplay, and just a minimum of dramatics that night.

resolving this conflict in his mind and soul

I

I can picture old Hank now sitting at the typer. Drinking from a bottle of cheap wine, Indian cigarette dangling from his thin lips, listening to Shostakovich on the radio, musing about losing his faith in women, looking in the mirror and smiling at his big head, his gray hair, his scraggly beard, his yellowing teeth, the hairs protruding from his nose and ears. "More wine," he mutters. "Lots more wine."

He recalls his friend, a writer of some renown, who wrote about wandering around Paris, happily anesthetized, advising him not to drink alone.

"Why not?" Hank asks the writer of some renown.

"Because it's undignified."

"Says who?"

"Says me."

"Well, I'm afraid we have a difference of opinion."

"Well, I'm afraid my opinion is the only opinion that matters," the writer of some renown says, fingering his Jesus dying on the cross necklace.

That's when Hank suddenly realizes what a phony the writer of some renown really is.

"You know," Hank says. "I used to think you really knew a thing or two about masturbating the word to orgasm. Granted, I couldn't understand half of what you were writing about, but you did it with such aplomb that I gave you the benefit of the doubt. But now…" He can't even complete his thought.

"I'm sorry you feel that way, Hank," says the writer of some renown. "I just feel like drinking should be a communal activity."

"Jesus, what the hell happened to you? You used to be so goddamn innovative. Now all you do is sit around with your Asian girlfriends drinking wine and painting your little watercolors. What about The Word?

What about trying to shove it up the ass of the Literary Establishment? You've gone soft, Henry!"

The writer of some renown scratches his earlobe and smiles sadly. "Hank... I'm an old man...I've had way too many colonoscopys...I limp...I forget shit all the time...when I get up out of a chair, I feel like the lower half of my body is completely paralyzed...I have cataracts...I can't hear very well...as for The Word and shoving it up the ass of the Literary Establishment...been there, done that, never got near the Pulitzer...I'm done, Hank...and if I wanna spend my time fucking Asian girls and drinking a couple bottles of Shiraz a day and painting water colors of your *ass*, then goddamn it, that's what I'm gonna do."

"It ain't over yet," Hank says.

"The difference between you and me, Hank, is I'm not interested in trying to uncover or discover the answers to Life's Most Complex Questions anymore. Truth-seeking is for the young. And the idealistic. And the ignorant. And when I say it's over, I mean that that part of the journey is over for me. I don't care about fighting the world any more. I don't care about examining mine or anybody else's existential crises. If that makes me shallow or lazy or a communist or a senile old man, so be it."

II

That night, Hank is bent over his typer writing a poem about agony, confusion, horror, fear, and ignorance, when the phone rings.

"Mr. Chinaski?"

"Uh heh?"

"Henry's gone," says a soft voice.

"Gone where?"

"He's dead."

"Well, shit, I was just with him."

"Yes, I know."

"What happened?"

"His heart."

"That figures."

"Mr. Chinaski, Henry wanted me to tell you that he thought you were one of the finest writers he's ever known. And that he hoped you wouldn't give up like him. He said you'd know what he was talking about."

"I do."

There is a pretty lengthy pause, which gives them both a little time to breathe.

"Well, I just thought you'd like to know, Mr. Chinaski," says the soft voice.

"Do you mind telling me who you are?"

"I'm his nurse."

"Oh really?"

"Yes, sir."

God, Hank thinks, the man was an invalid and was still getting as much pussy as ever. God love him.

"Well, thanks for letting me know," Hank says, and he hangs up.

I can picture old Hank now. Gulping the last of his wine, studying a self-portrait he painted the night before of him drinking alone and wondering how he can make it more dignified.

It's perfect just as it is, he thinks, and continues working on another blunt-edged attack on his embattled and seemingly impossible relationship with his former self.

the fabled, the forgotten

I was up on stage playing my guitar, singing youthful, irreverent anthems. The crowds were small, but not completely unappreciative. Many of them were drunk, divorced, alone, or unemployed. They put on calm faces and nodded their heads to the rhythm of my strum, even when my lyrics were as insightful as a fallen god.

When a song ended, they would usually applaud. Most had big broad smiles. Some slept. Others wept. With every chord I played, I just followed what was in me.

Then one night I added a harmonica to my act and wrote on my guitar, THIS MACHINE KILLS FACISTS, just like Woody Guthrie, and people became teary-eyed and emotional and I suddenly became me, in spite of myself, and the pressure of being me kept me going.

any spectrum of women in today's society

My point is this. That I had something to say, but not much. I was relying too much on my thesaurus. Reading too many Cliff notes.

The women in my life were telling me things like: "I dated this really intellectual writer guy who would gaze into my eyes. Eventually, I realized that he wasn't looking into my soul, he was trying to remember who I was."

The men in my life weren't saying anything at all.

Even though I was a born progressive human secularist, I converted to alcoholism in my late thirties.

In the mid-eighties, I hitchhiked to Cali in a pea-green Volkswagen bus with a feme sole. She was forty-three. A waitress. Likable enough. Had a navel ring and corn rows.

In Chandler, Oklahoma, she confessed to me that she whiled away the hours by watching Sesame Street and taking a yellow highlighter to the King James Bible.

I don't think we were in love, or even in lust, but we sure as hell knew how to be dishonest with each other.

While lying in bed at a Motel 6 in Gallop, New Mexico, she sighed heavily and said, "I've always felt I was original, shy and reserved, but not reclusive."

We did fuck that night. And it was memorable. There should have been a shrine built to her ass.

She had a presence and toughness about her, a real vampy-New York-hip-art-rock kind of thing going on.

She was a Jim Carroll poem without the emotion and she brought forward the fact that a woman always needs a hook in this life.

the most genius solutions

I
Jon Jon's wearing black shades in order to hide his bloodshot eyes; he's been smoking a lot of pot lately and doesn't have any eye drops.

"It's a fine line between education and ignorance," he says to somebody standing in line with him at the Workforce Development Center.

The somebody nods his head and says, "You got that right."

II
Jon Jon's job counselor has major attitude. He'll get no coddling from her, no nurturing, no words of encouragement, not even any tough love, just a couple of job leads for him to follow up on. One of them is a customer service associate for an airline. The other's a manufacturing job for a tobacco company.

"Apply online," his counselor tells him, pointing to a bank of computers against the wall.

"Got some things to take care of first," Jon Jon says. "I'll be back."

The counselor doesn't say anything. Her silence says it all.

III
Outside, Jon Jon runs into the somebody he was conversing with in line, a middle-aged man wearing a floppy hat and a poncho, smoking a White Owl Peach Sport.

"My life's kinda like limbo without the doing or dying," the man says.

Jon Jon nods, says, "Well, brother, it's no easier at ground zero," and walks to the bus stop where he meets a girl named Sandy. Smoking Dunhills. Drinking Southern Comfort with a splash of lime out of a thermos. Mascara running. Throaty laugh. Eyes without a past. Lips painted purplish-red. Necklace bought at a Stuckey's in New Mexico.

She turns to Johnny and says: "Sometimes when I come upon a stranger I have the urge to kick them; especially when they're at their most vulnerable. When they're bending down to tie a child's shoe lace or confined to a wheel chair or forced to walk with a cane or a walker or studying quietly at a table in the library or just after having been given some horrible news or standing in line at the unemployment office or struggling to carry some heavy object or involved in a deep prayer or having just been discharged from the hospital after undergoing major surgery or while they're crying or being born or dying. That's when I fantasize about kicking them as hard as I can. And then I realize I'm not alone in thinking those thoughts. And I'm at peace with myself again."

Jon Jon smiles and winks. "Sister," he says. "This life ain't nothin' but a crapshoot," and he boards the number 27 bus.

When he arrives at his destination, he notices some graffiti written on the bus shelter poster: "In the middle of the journey of our life I came to myself within a dark wood where the straight way was lost."

Jon Jon gets off the bus, lights a cigarette, walks toward the library to check out Knut Hanson's *Hunger.*

just another easy-to-believe tragicomedy

Think it was 1990.

Funny how you can't remember dates when you've been alone for so long.

Seems like somebody was always pulling a gun on me in those days. Something about sleeping with women I wasn't supposed to be sleeping with. Fortunately, I never got shot. Little muscle pain every now and then. But that's why they invented aspirin.

Eventually, I'd move on.

Usually meet some woman with a flushed face and puffy eyes living in a sleepyheaded little town, not unlike some of those burgs in Cheshire County, New Hampshire.

She'd ask about my past and I'd shrug a little and mumble something about "kicking a dead horse," and she'd look at me like I had no sense of humor and wonder who the hell this American stereotype was; but somehow we'd always end up locked in a static embrace after trying to achieve a higher form of bliss.

Come morning, she'd wake up with neck pain from using my knee cap as a pillow and I'd have cramps from attempting to perform one of those tantric techniques, so we'd take a non-habit forming prescription pain killer, because that's what they were invented for, and spend the rest of the day determining which one of us could go through a needle's eye without overdosing.

We'd come down off an inauthentic high a few hours later and she'd ask me some trick question like, "So, what did you, ditch your inert and restless life in search of a more authentic experience?"

I'd show a polite grin and say something like, "Just on a one-man mission to find something morally positive," and she'd sort of accept that, but I could tell she'd be thinking I was just another one of those t-shirted slackers trying like hell to break away from his family's pathological path. And she was right. Always searching for the ring of truth by going down blind alleys, always ending up stranded in the middle of a mythic American dream.

Then she'd go into the kitchen and start mixing screwdrivers in those little juice boxes and I'd go off on another one of my lonesome ruminations and suddenly begin not to trust my memory at all.

She'd return twenty minutes later, drained and pale, hand me my drink, glance anxiously at the clock, force a smile, say, "I've always felt I was capable of great friendships and kindnesses. But I am strange. I do come from a different place."

Suddenly, her eyes would fill with tears and I'd reach out and take her hand. "Well, at least you're not somebody whose worldview is often obscured by an inability to fathom much of anything, like me," I'd say and she'd smile and make some comment like, "So much dysfunction and chaos in our backstories, man, so much existential absurdity."

As usual, I'd have no comment, no argument, and wouldn't even feel guilty about it.

There'd be a silent but perceptible grinding of teeth there and with that, she'd lock the door, and we'd go back to bed.

Because that's what beds were invented for.

among the everywoman

Maybe I was just trying to figure you out and ravage your body the way time has ravaged it.

Or maybe I was just attempting to make conversation with your lips and persuade you to reopen old festering wounds and share your closed heart with an open heart surgeon who would rather be operating on your brain, because that's where the real skill lies.

Or maybe I was alone without a candle in the dark and didn't have the wherewithal to whistle while I cursed the wick and forgot to celebrate the flint as I watched my lady's flinty heart dimming in that fingernail in the sky moon.

Or maybe I was neither in love nor in lust; I was just alone and nonplused and unwilling to put up much of a fuss when you opened your lovin' vein with that blunt instrument called your brain and let it spill out all over my golden-black flame of hair and drip beneath my astigmatic stare.

Or maybe my mouth ejaculated when my tongue should have been on a leash and maybe I unleashed my id when my superego should have been refereeing and when my ego was taking a selfie in front of my looking-glass self.

Or maybe the blame lies with the lie of a shy guy treading enigmatically in front of the Sphinx and musing in front of his muses as Medusa washes the original serpent of sin from her reptile coif with an anti-venom made from the blood of Christ and displays her scarred neck for Perseus and celebrates her disembodiment from a netherworld that eschews phantasmagoria and prevents her from throwing stones at glass ceilings.

my bohemian life in brooklyn

Penniless theater major chain-smokes cigarillos and extinguishes them in a can of Red Bull, tightens her arms around her torso, making sure too much of her psychological motives doesn't escape.

Always on some collision course, something always getting in her way; laziness, booze, drugs, it's all written somewhere in her DNA, nurture, nature, who the hell can wrap their mind around any of that shit, anyway?

"I swear," she says, choking up, leaving the thought unfinished.

"Please," I say, sucking on an unlit cigarette. "Don't compare yourself to Amy Winehouse tonight. Let's just celebrate your sublime inner torment by remaining tight-lipped and stoic, shall we?"

Her shoulders remain drooped with the collective weight of The Actors Studio. "There are so many subtle allusions to a lot of different things going on here," she says.

As I struggle to replicate my square-jawed ruggedness, she remains aloof, almost unreadable, turns on the TV, and settles in to watching some banal chick-flick that fails to produce any innovative ideas and is laughably formulaic.

There will be no more breathtaking responses to my trite questions because she's had enough of my direction for tonight.

open phones

Let's wander over here to Don. Don, you're on the air.

Hi, Dr. Ginger, how are you?

Very well, thank you.

I'm sorry, I'm a little nervous...

No need to apologize for being nervous.

(slight chuckle) Alright.

What's going on, Don?

Well, I'm in trouble, I think. A little trouble, err...

What sort of trouble?

I don't know if it's trouble or not.

Either you're in trouble or you're not in trouble, Don, which is it?

I got a girl pregnant.

Ah-hah.

Two, actually.

Two? You got two women pregnant?

Yes, ma'am.

Are you married?

Yes I am.

Is one of the pregnant women your wife, by any chance?

Neither of them are.

Ohhkay! Isn't that interesting?

(nervous laugh) Uhh yaa…

You know something, Don?

What's that?

I was wrong. You *should* be nervous.

I know.

How did all this play out?

Well…

You can't keep your pecker in your pants?

It's not that I can't keep it in my pants.

Of course it is. If you're married and you got two other women pregnant, you can't keep your pecker in your pants. That's just simple mathematics, Don, no?

In a way, I guess.

"In a way," you "guess?" Don…

Yes.

Are you just so fine that women can't keep their hands off you? Are you that fine?

I'm alright.

You're alright.

Yeah.

How old are you, Don?

Thirty-four.

Kids?

Two.

Oyy.

I know.

So if you know…never mind. Who are these other women? How did you happen to meet them?

I just meet women throughout the course of the day.

So where did you meet them?

(pause) At a bar.

A bar?

Yes ma'am.

You're thirty-four years old, you're married, you have two kids, what are you doing frequenting bars, Don?

I like to go to them every now and then.

You don't go to bars. When you're married with children, you do not go to bars, unless you're with your wife, do you understand that?

My wife lets me.

Your wife does not let you go to bars by yourself.

She told me it was alright.

Don, are you telling me the truth?

Yes ma'am.

Why don't I believe that? Do you know why I don't believe that, Don?

No ma'am.

Because I'm a woman and there is no way in hell I would allow my husband to go to a bar by himself.

Yes ma'am.

You know what, Don? I think you're lying. Why are you lying to me?

Well…

Are you lying to me? (pause) Don, answer my question, are you lying to me?

No, I'm not lying.

So your wife…what sort of wife do you have? What kind of woman is she? Are you telling me…does she go to bars by herself?

No ma'am.

So we have a little double-standard going on in your relationship, don't we, Don? In other words, what's good for the goose ain't so good for the gander, is that what you're saying?

No ma'am.

So why don't you let her go to bars by herself?

Because she can't.

What do you mean, she can't? Why can't she?

She's a quadriplegic.

(pause) Ohh…Well, you didn't tell me that.

Yes ma'am.

Now I understand. I don't approve of it, but I understand.

Yes ma'am.

But in the meantime, two other women are pregnant by you.

Yes ma'am.

That you met in a bar.

Yes ma'am.

Don?

Yes ma'am?

Stop calling me "ma'am." It's really annoying me.

Sorry about that.

(a sigh) I don't know what to say to you, Don.

I know.

I mean, I know what to *say* to you, but the question is, are you ready to *hear* what I have to say to you?

Yes ma'am. I mean, I think so.

You know I think you're scum, Don. You know that.

I believe I do.

And that I think you ought to rot in hell for eternity. You're aware of that.

Absolutely.

Having said that…Are you prepared to support these children, Don?

If I have to.

Mm mm, you didn't listen to the question. Are you prepared to support them?

(pause) Well…?

I didn't think so. And the women you impregnated? Are they prepared to become mothers?

I didn't ask them.

(an incredulous chuckle) Well, Don, what the hell have you been doing since you found out you're going to be a baby daddy again? (no reply) Hello? Don?

I'm here.

I don't think you *are* here. I think you're very much on another planet in a galaxy far, far away right now, hoping that this whole thing will just blow over and these women will just magically disappear from your life forever. Maybe they will, I don't know them. Or maybe your seed is just so damn desirable that women are knockin' themselves over tryin' to get themselves some because they know their children are going to grow up to be geniuses. Is this possible?

I don't know about that.

You're right, I don't know about that, either, Don. Here's my suggestion. Get another job. An extremely well-paying job. I also want you to tell your wife.

You think?

Do I think, Don? Were you not gonna mention the fact that you knocked-up a couple of sluts?

I hadn't made up my mind one way or the other.

Well, I've just made up your mind for you, OK?

OK.

You're unbelievable, Don.

You're right.

Of course I'm right. Now get outta here. I'm gonna get fired if I keep talking to you.

Thanks.

Don't thank me. Just pray that your wife doesn't put a hit out on you. I'll be back after the news. If you're lucky. Jesus, can you believe out of eight million sperm, that guy won? Pathetic, absolutely pathetic. Lord, help us.

it's about removing the layers

I did a few things differently this Thanksgiving. First of all I shaved. I also put the store-bought chocolate-pecan pie into a glass pie plate instead of bringing it to Nana's house in its original plastic container. It's all about the illusion. I didn't fool anybody by relocating the pie, though, because my family knows that my past performances are almost always an indicator for how to predict my future performances.

Nevertheless, I still felt I'd upped my game considerably, particularly since I'd given myself such a close, smooth shave. Ordinarily I show up with a growth on my face as unruly as my Uncle Sol's chest hairs, while donning black polyester pants, a white tee shirt, a sheepskin vest, leather flip flops, and a khaki fishing cap with a few lewers dangling from the brim.

This year, however, I kept it simple and wore a plain embroidered kaftan and a pair of cheap sandals. You just can't beat the comfort.

Dinner conversation with my family has always been an oblique and opaque experience, and this year's dialogue was certainly no exception.

Before the Tofurky was even sliced, Nana was mentioning her fondness for dark rooms, drawn curtains, black walls, and staying under the covers. "My mood sank so low," she said. "I was admitted into a sanitarium and was treated for melancholia. Do they still call them sanitariums these days? Do they still call it melancholia?"

There was a silence as long as our faces.

Then Sis, who sometimes has a knack for saving the day, said, "They do. I'm sure somewhere they do."

But it was Papa who topped us all.

"I've converted to Christianity," he said. "I've also become an Eagle Scout."

"He's joking," Nana said.

"The hell I am," Papa said, storming out of the room and returning with his Eagle Scout medal, a burlap bag with something moving inside of it, and an autographed copy of pastor Joel Osteen's book, *Your Best Life Now*.

"Does it look like I'm joking now?" Papa said.

Nana looked at Papa for a few seconds and then moved her gaze toward the rest of us. "He's had too much schnapps."

"Oh yeah?" Papa said. And suddenly his eyes rolled back into his head and he began speaking in tongues.

"Mamzer mashugga megillah nafkeh narish nisht geyfloygen nishtgutnick nudnik nudjen kaneh chazzer chazzerei ech mir!"

Then Papa reached into the burlap bag, pulled out a garter snake and began handling it.

"Shlimazel schleppen shlecht veib plagen pitshetsh pisk-malocheh!"

Nana shook her head. "He's not speaking in tongues," she said. "He's speaking in Yiddish."

Then Nana started yelling at him in Yiddish.

The only phrase from her entire tirade I understood was, "You moron, you're supposed to use poisonous snakes" and I'm pretty sure she called Joel Osteen a charlatan and accused Papa of being a self-hating Jew.

Then Papa said he'd been schtuping some thirty-four year old Bible school teacher from New Rochelle for the last year and a half and how his soul had been delivered ever since she introduced him to the 700 Club with Pat Robertson, and besides, he was goddam sick and tired of being thought of as a Christ-killer and that was why he converted and dammit, if he wanted to convert, that was his own goddam business, and if we didn't like it, we could all go to hell!

Well, what was there to say to that?

We all just sat there.

Even the snake.

Three or four minutes later, sis attempted to employ one of her famous tactical diversions. "Who wants pie?"

But nobody said anything.

Nana stood up from the table, picked up her plate, brought it into the kitchen, set it in the sink, and began scrubbing some pots and pans.

Papa pulled a flask of schnapps from an inside pocket of his jacket, took a strong swig, and returned it to his pocket. "Let this be a lesson to you all," he said.

Sis gave him her famous confused look. "And what lesson would that be?"

"If you have to ask, then you haven't learned it yet." Papa said, putting on his hat and coat and walking out the door.

As Sis sliced up that store-bought chocolate pecan pie served in the glass pie plate, the snake slithered back into the burlap bag.

And I thought, next year I'm just going to stay home and eat one of those Swanson Hungry Man turkey breast dinners and I'll probably serve it on Wedgwood China, just for the hell of it.

a trivial, tedious clock

She thinks it's so sad that all he does is sit around reading and watching TV all day.

"Why is that sad?" he says. "It's what I've wanted to do since I was in high school!"

She just thinks he should be around people more.

He says he's not interested in being around anyone.

She sighs, retracts.

Then, a final dig. "I hate who you've become," she says, as she walks into the kitchen to water her plants.

stronger than you think

A lot has changed.
I have changed.
Now there's no in between.
It's either a yes or a no.

what if?

Got an email. "Like your writing. Have a film project I'd like you to work on. Call me. Billy Buda."

So I called him.

After he finished listing the "numerous indie sleeper hits" he'd co-produced over the years that included titles like *The Secret of The Psychedelic Policewoman*, *Battle of the Colossal Bee* and *The Sensual Touch of Sherlock Holmes, Part V*, he instructed me to meet him at Denny's at the corner of Third and Bulldyke and to bring a pad and a pencil because "we got work to do, bubela."

Buda was a small, wiry, all-black-wearing opportunist with a bald head full of razor rash and a handshake reminiscent of an unconscious halibut.

The third or fourth thing out of his mouth was, "Want you to write a coupla black lesbian characters that are gonna get it on during some course of the story...don't care when, don't care how, but I wanna see 'em in the sack before the end of the movie, OK?"

"Well. I guess I can finagle something."

"No no, don't guess. Guessing is a word I am not familiar or comfortable with. If you're gonna work with me you'll need to know my vocabulary, it's vital."

"Alright."

"No guessing, no maybes, no trying, no thinking about doing it, ya unnerstand? You can, you will, you must, end of discussion."

"Absolutely."

"Nuther thing I'm partial to is interracial relationships between white guys and black women. And I don't mean light-skinned women. African-black. Black as coal, black as tar black women. It's a passion of mine. And not only a sexual one. I was in the streets in the sixties during that whole civil rights brou ha ha singin' 'We Shall Overcome' along with everybody else and being a Jew, I've always sort of aligned myself with black causes and I know where they're coming from. So, what do you think of it so far?"

I thought about it so far. "Of what so far?"

"The premise. Can you do anything with it?"

"You haven't told me what the premise is."

"I told you. Black lesbians and interracial relationships!"

"Well, no disrespect to you, Billy, but it doesn't really give me much to go on."

"Do you want this gig?"

"Yes, of course I want the gig."

"'Cuz I'll get Joe Eszterhas on the phone right now and ask him."

"I'll do the gig. I just thought you already had a premise in mind, something mapped out."

"Uhm, excuse me, is it my job to map things out for you?"

"No."

"Would you like to know what my job as a producer is?"

"I know what your job is."

"My job is to put together a package."

"I realize that."

He counted on his fingers. "It is to find a director, a writer, and a star. That, in a nutshell, is my job."

"I understand."

"Your job is to write a screenplay. It's not my job to 'map' things out. It's not my job to delineate every plot point, every story beat, every character nuance, every obligatory scene, every climax. That's *your* job. Are we straight?"

"We're straight."

"Good. Now brainstorm me, throw some ideas at me, what can you do with it?"

"I can't work this way, Billy."

"What do you mean you can't work this way?"

"Let me go home, sit down at my typewriter and think about it. I work best that way."

"Are you gonna cop that prima donna shit with me? Because if you are, Alan Smithee's available for this project."

"How many writers do you usually work with?"

"Depends on the project. Sometimes you need a little tweaking, a little punching up. Your strength may be dialogue, somebody else is good with plot, another guy's good with structure, it depends."

"So I'm gonna be one of God knows how many others?"

"Look it, you gimme a draft that knocks me on my ass, I guarantee you, you'll be the only writer. If, on the other hand, you gimme one that's forty, fifty, sixty percent there."

"I'm not naive. I know how the game is played, but."

"You'll get screen credit, the Writer's Guild requires that."

"I know that!"

"What if it's shit? Is that what you're worried about? Too many cooks in the kitchen and you're left with the screen credit?"

"No, of course not, nooh."

"That's the chance you take, bubela, you know that as well as I."

"But, Billy...I need more than just black lesbians and interracial relationships."

"They made a whole friggin' movie from one image in 1939. Do you know what that image was?"

"What was that?"

"It was the image of a seventy foot ape on top of the Empire State Building."

"'King Kong.'"

"You're goddamn right! 'King' fucking 'Kong.' The guy who wrote 'King Kong' had to build an entire story around one image! Was that a lot to work with? You talk about a challenge! I've given you more than *that* to work with!"

"He had 'Beauty and the Beast' to work with as a..."

"Regardless of what he had to work with, the schmuck had to come up with a way to get a seventy foot ape up the friggin' Empire State Building! Are you listening to me? Don't give me that shit you need more to work with, you're a better writer than that!"

"OK."

"Whaddaya think, I'm shootin' for an Oscar here, for chrissakes? We'll be lucky if this thing goes straight to video! Russ Myers was an *auteur* compared to the director I hired, alright? I'm not asking you to write *Citizen Kane*, for Chrissakes!"

"I understand."

"It's business! This is not art! You want art, go work with Merchant and Ivory. Or whichever one of 'em's still alive! Why, you gettin' cold feet now?"

"Noo."

"Are you comfortable with the assignment?"

"Yeah, I'm cool."

"I want a first draft in three weeks."

"Fine."

"Jesus, I was bluffing. Are you serious? You can do it in three weeks?"

"Why not?"

"That's what I'm saying."

Buda's cell phone rang. "Hello?" he said. "Gretchen! The lovely Gretchen, how are you?...Ahh, you know, the usual boundary issues and the overwhelming lack of self-esteem to deal with, but other than that...Can the Good Doc see me today?...Great! Three o'clock is perfect! I appreciate the call back, love. Alrighty, bye bye..." He folded the phone. "I'm gonna get this chick."

"Who?"

"My analyst's secretary. She is gorgeous."

"You see an analyst?"

"I figure I don't smoke, I don't drink, I don't do drugs, I might as well have some kind of crutch."

"Is it helping?"

"I don't know, but I get to write it off. So are we straight? You need anything else from me?"

I thought about it. "I don't think so."

"Awesome. See ya in three weeks."

I went home, sat down at the typewriter, stared at the blank sheet of paper for an hour and a half, and decided it was time I started seeing an analyst.

the bubble dancer

I've worked a lot of odd jobs and with some pretty odd people, but, man, that first job was a doozy.

There was a little fish restaurant called The Captain's Cabin that'd been there for like a hundred years or more and they were looking for a dishwasher.

One of my buddies was working there during the summer but had to leave because he was going off to study philosophy or something at some college in upstate New York.

He said it was a pretty cool place to work because sometimes the cooks gave you beers after they closed, even if you were underage.

I figured that was my kind of place, so I went over there and filled out an application and the hostess, who looked like she'd been there for a hundred years or more herself, told me she'd see if the owner was available to interview me.

I was a kind of nervous and needed something to do with my hands, so I picked up a menu and opened it.

There was a little message in there from the "Executive Chef and Owner."

I guess he wanted everybody who ate there to who the hell he was.

"Hi, folks," is how his message began. I thought that was sort of a corny way to kick things off, but oh well.

"My name Is Anton Cooper. I'm a self-taught chef. I've always been fascinated with food and people's relationship to it. To me, food has always meant love and I always seem to have a very intense, visceral experience whenever I'm around it. Whether I'm enjoying a three-course meal at a French restaurant or making myself a Fluffernutter sandwich in my kitchen at home!"

Who was he kidding with that crap?

"I bought this restaurant two years ago because I wanted a place where I could hang my toque! Well, I'm pleased to say that my toque is still hanging here and that it is quite happy and proud to be doing so. As the great American chef and food writer James Beard said, 'Food is our common ground, a universal experience.' Bon Appétit."

I have really bad memories of that phrase, bon appétit, because the last person who said it to me was my grandmother and she said it just before serving me her infamous tuna noodle casserole and I ended up being rushed to the hospital with food poisoning.

The hostess returned a couple minutes later. Her breathing was kind of heavy and she looked a little pissed off.

"Chef'll be out in just a minute," she said. "My name's Trudy. If you ever need anything, come see me," and she headed back toward where she came from.

She said it like she was the one that ran the place.

I found out later she practically did.

About a half hour later, a big burly guy with a buzz cut and a full beard came in from outside holding a bandana and wearing a wrinkled chef's uniform that had all kinds of stains on the jacket and a few holes in the pants.

He looked pretty rough, like he was hung over since 1969.

"Hey," he said. "I'm Anton. Have a seat."

But I was already sitting.

"Lot goin' on, man," he said, collapsing into one of the nearby chairs. "Lot goin' on…"

Boy, his eyes were blood shot.

I'm pretty sure he was either drunk or stoned or both.

And he smelled of booze, fish, and cigarettes.

I'm already not too crazy about fish.

I could sort of handle the booze and the cigarettes.

But it was the smell of fish that really made me want to gag.

"So you wanna be a dishwasher," Anton said.

Like it was my life's ambition or something.

"Well, I need a job and a friend of mine used to work here."

"Oh yeah? Who's that?"

"Jimmy Moreski."

"Oh yeah, Jimbo. Good kid. Hard worker, too. Hated to lose him. College bound. Education's important. He'll do well…"

"Yeah," I said.

"Know anything about this business?" Anton said.

"I know about James Beard. He's my mother's favorite chef. She loves his recipes."

"Really. Me, too. Great improviser. Knew when to stray from a recipe."

"That's what my mom says," I lied. What the hell did I have to lose?

"Well, lemme tell ya a little about me, what I'm like to work for. I can be a real prick. I don't have time to be holding anybody's hand. I'll show you something once, maybe twice, depending on how I'm feeling that day. But if you ask me a third time, I'm-a show you the door."

Jimmy had already schooled me on Anton. He said he could be a little ornery, but he was cool as long as you did your job and didn't ask him too many questions.

He told me some other things about him, too.

The only thing Jimmy didn't tell me about Anton was how much he loved to talk about himself.

He was going on and on about all these cooking techniques and how he backpacked across France when he was seventeen and took classes with some four-star French chef who'd cooked for a royal family from Croatia and blah blah blah.

I stopped listening to him after that.

What did I care if he'd won some cook-off in Seattle, Washington for his braised veal and lamb shanks?

I was there to apply for a friggin' job as a dishwasher.

So I just sat there, like I always do whenever I'm forced to listen to somebody's vocal ejaculations, and thought about some memories from my childhood.

I must have thought about thirty or forty different memories before I started paying attention to Anton again, who was still talking.

"I mean, we're all pretty much fucking cursed, aren't we? We all have demons and shit wreaking havoc inside of our heads. We're literally dying a little every single day, I mean, that's life, isn't it? What is that saying? 'Into each life a little rain must fall?' What was that, from the Bible or something? I honestly think it's like totally fucking amazing that people live as long as they do, given all the pain and disappointment and bitterness and anger and shit they're forced to endure, you know? Anyway, I'm off point. I'm a very passionate guy. I'm just lucky I found cooking. I have this saying. Well, I sorta borrowed it from somebody, but... Mine is not to reason why. Mine is but to cook and die. That's my philosophy, man, right there."

And then he went into this trance or something.

He was just caught up in something.

Probably thinking about some memory from childhood like me, who knows?

A couple minutes later he came out of it and looked at me with those blood-shot eyes and said, "So when can you start?"

I started the next day because Anton said he was desperate.

Too bad he wasn't desperate enough to pay me more than $5.50 an hour.

But what the hell, I got one free meal a day and two if I worked a double shift.

And every now and then, Peter, the sous chef, would give me a beer after work.

If he was in a good mood.

Which wasn't too often.

Peter was one of those guys who'd started working in the restaurant business when he was about my age and just stayed.

When I met him, he was in his mid-thirties and looked like a rolling stone that had stopped rolling because it didn't have anywhere else to roll.

He'd come in, probably stoned, with a beer in one hand and a Camel stud in the other, always singing something by Frank Sinatra or Dean Martin or Bing Crosby.

Which was kind of funny because he didn't look the kind of guy who'd be singing "Strangers in the Night" or "You're Nobody 'till Somebody Loves You" or "White Christmas".

He looked like the kind of guy who'd be singing something by Black Sabbath or The Rolling Stones or Alice Cooper.

He liked those bands, too.

But he never sang any of their songs; just the ones by those old crooners.

I never had any problems with Peter.

You just had to watch his moods.

You had to watch Anton's moods, too, but I never really worked with him because he usually opened the restaurant and worked the lunch shift.

I'd get there around four.

He'd always be in his office and the door would be locked.

One day Peter took me aside and told me the reason Anton always locked the door to his office was because he was smoking crack.

That was one of the other things Jimmy Moreski had told me about Anton.

But I didn't want to tell Peter I'd already heard about that so I just said, "Wow, really?"

"And he owes a lot of back taxes. He borrowed money from the old lady, the hostess."

"Trudy?" I said.

"Like ten grand."

"Are you serious?"

He said Anton still owed Uncle Sam something like fifteen or twenty grand.

And that he wasn't just smoking crack.

He was also selling it.

"And that's not all he's selling." He lowered his voice even more. "All those rich, lonely widows comin' in for lunch? They're not just comin' here for his Yankee Pot Roast."

Then he walked away singing, "I'm just a gigolo and everywhere I go, People know the part I'm playin'. Pay for every dance, sellin' each romance, Ooohh what they're sayin'?"

I heard all kinds of rumors about Anton after that.

He'd borrowed money from a Mexican drug kingpin.

He was a white supremacist.

He'd killed a man.

He was fucking the waitresses.

He was fucking the waiters.

He was fucking Trudy.

Apparently, the only ones he wasn't fucking were me and Peter.

I couldn't have cared less if Anton was fucking dead gay Mexican supremacist waitresses.

As long as he cut me a check every two weeks and it didn't bounce, we were cool.

I was a dishwasher.

I wasn't there to start any shit.

I guess that's why people like talking to me.

They know I'm just going to listen to them and keep my mouth shut.

One time Anton told me practically his entire life story.

I'll never forget it.

Peter had called in sick so Anton had to fill in for him.

I'd gotten there at my usual time.

Even from the parking lot, I could hear Anton screaming like a madman.

He was always good for at least one or two loud outbursts a day.

Someone or something was always pissing him off.

Especially the wait staff.

So I didn't really give it much thought.

Until I heard doors slam and saw Kim, one of the waitresses, making a beeline for her car.

"What's going on?" I said.

"Don't go in there," she said. "He's fucking crazy!"

"What else is new?" I said.

She shook her head in disgust, got in her car and sped off.

As I headed toward the side entrance that lead directly into the kitchen, I could see Anton through the windows in the door, kicking and punching walls and throwing pots and pans and utensils across the room and screaming like a damn maniac.

It was actually pretty funny.

If only I'd had a video camera.

Especially for the next thing that happened.

I couldn't believe it.

He actually started boxing with the wall.

The concrete wall.

Just really punching the shit out of it; looking like one of those ramshackle boxers who were hired to throw a fight but changed their mind halfway through the third round.

"Fucker, that's the *last* time you're callin' in sick! That's the *last* time, you stupid piece a shit! I oughta fire your fuckin' ignorant ass! This shit drives me *crazy!*"

Then he pulled his arm back and punched the wall as hard as he could.

At least it looked like it was as hard as he could.

I'm not a physicist, so I don't really know.

But I know after he punched the wall he doubled over and staggered around for a few seconds before falling to the ground like one of his cakes.

I kind of felt sorry for the dude; the way he was sprawled out on the floor and whimpering like a chef who'd just punched a concrete wall with his closed, hard fist because his sous-chef had called in sick.

I thought about calling in sick myself at that point.

But I would have been docked and I was starting to like having a little walking around money, so I played dumb and pretended like I hadn't seen Anton punching the wall.

When I walked into the kitchen, Anton looked up at me and shouted, "Get outta here! Leamme alone."

I could tell her was a little drunk.

"What happened, man?" I said, kneeling down beside him.

"Fuckin' Peter called in sick…and Bobby's on vacation."

"You alright?"

"Never better."

"Your hand looks a little messed-up. Maybe you should go to the emergency room."

"I don't have any health insurance."

"They still gotta treat you."

"It's just a little bruise."

"You gonna be able to cook with your hand like that?"

"I've cooked with a broken arm, I can sure as hell cook with a hand like this."

"What about J.D.? Maybe he could come in and help?"

J.D. was the pantry chef.

"I fired him."

"When?"

"Today."

"Why?"

"He pissed me off! He plated a dessert wrong. The Key Lime Soufflé with Raspberry Chambord. He forgot the fucking garnish! The fresh raspberries and a thinly sliced lime wedge. It's a fucking Key Lime Soufflé With Raspberry Chambord, for Chrise sakes! And he knows this! 'Well, I forgot to order the raspberries and the limes,' he says. Oh that's great! That's beautiful! You fucking moron! 'Well, people don't really know the difference.' Yes, they do, J.D.! They do know the difference. People are *very* well aware. They look at the dessert menu and see we have Key Lime Soufflé with Raspberry Chambord and assume that limes and raspberries are somehow gonna be involved, you ignorant fucking moron! What, you thought you were just gonna slip it by me without me noticing? Nobody's gonna be working in my kitchen and short-cutting it like that. I don't care how talented you think you are. I don't care how many fucking classes you took at Johnson and Wales. You don't fuck with me, OK? This is my restaurant! *Mine!* And then he comes to me, couple months ago, balling like a little girl. 'I need more money, man, I need more money, I'm barely makin' it on what you're payin' me, I gotta baby on the way, can't you give me some kind of a raise, something?' So I said, yeah, OK, I'll give you a raise. But you're gonna start taking on more responsibilities. You're gonna order all the produce from now on. 'Oh, that's not a problem, that's not a problem, I can do that.' Can ya? *Really?* So why didn't you order the fucking raspberries and the limes? 'I forgot, man, I'm sorry.' You know what? I'm sorry, too, but you're fired! I can't be dealing with that kind of shit! I'm in debt up to my fucking neck! Tryna save this place from going under! And I'm surrounded by fucking retards! Whaddaya want from me, man? What the hell do ya want from me? You stupid jackass!"

Then he started crying.

That was a little awkward.

I mean, what do you say to your crying boss?

Probably best not to say anything at all.

So I just sat there.

While he reminisced about his childhood.

Wow.

Forty-five minutes of him talking about his foster mother.

Which can be a very dangerous thing.

Particularly when you're drunk and just about demolished your hand.

"I never felt she took proper care of me," he said, quietly weeping. "She was always leaving me in the stroller in the middle of the park while she went off and got a drink at a local tavern with a casual male friend or traipsing to the nearest twenty-five to fifty percent off sale at the local women's discount store. She seemed to always be leaving me somewhere by myself or with irresponsible babysitters. There was Clare, a thirty-seven year old chain-smoking, alcoholic divorcee who sat around watching soap operas, game shows, eating Ding Dongs and corn chips and drinking Old Milwaukee beer. Whenever I asked her for something, she'd look at me, sneer, and say, 'You gotta shot, kid,' and go back to doing whatever it was she was doing, which was usually nothing. Then there was Joan, a forty-seven year old chain-smoking, alcoholic divorcee who'd recently found God and spent the majority of her time reading passages from the Bible and telling me, 'God doesn't like little boys who don't obey their babysitters and if you don't obey me, He's gonna send you straight to hell when you die.' But none of them could top Lucy, a fifty-seven year old former stripper and wheat germ fanatic, who served me brandy and pot brownies during each visit and explained the facts of life to me by making me watch the films of John Holmes. 'Now ya see how big he is?' she'd say. 'Big?' I'd say. 'His winkee; he's gotta very big winkee. See that?' 'Uh-heh?' 'Ladies like a man with a big winkee.' I'd never heard the term 'winkee' used in that context before. I just assumed she was talking about the man's eyes, that he had big eyes, and because he had big eyes and a big wink, I grew up believing women liked men with big eyes and big winks."

A few seconds later, he was asleep.

At least I was hoping he was asleep.

Just to make sure, I tapped him lightly on the shoulder and said, "Hey, Anton," and he raised the index finger on his good hand to his lips and shushed me and mumbled, "Few more minutes, mom... I'm so tired...I'm so damn tired."

That's when Trudy came into the kitchen.

When she saw Anton spread out on the floor like that, she almost dropped the bag of groceries she was holding.

"Oh my God, what in the world?"

I told her what happened.

"My goodness," Trudy said. "I was gone for twenty-minutes... He sent me to the store to pick up some limes and some raspberries. What is the matter with that man?"

Anton's arms and legs started twitching. "Fuck'em all," he said.

Trudy was really pissed.

She looked like she really wanted to curse him out.

"What a total waste of a..." she said. "I begged him to see a therapist."

She had a lot more she could have said; but she just shook her head and let out a sigh that I felt on my neck.

"Well, we're going to have to close for the night. We have no choice. You might as well go home."

I told her I didn't mind hanging around for a while.

"There's no need. I'll stay with him until he wakes up. *If* he wakes up."

"Anything you want me to do before I go?"

"Pray like hell," she said.

The next day, I got a call from Trudy telling me not to come in to work.

Anton had been arrested for tax evasion and possession and intent to sell and deliver drugs.

And I discovered the joys of unemployment insurance.

a revolutionary sense of truth

The tender old man
so frail in the midnight moon
waits for a new day.

curious about what's really small

Becca called her Mom two days after she'd left her fiancé at the altar. "How did Daddy propose to you?"

"Apparently, he had just came from a handball game. He came in in like a tee shirt and he was kind of sweaty and I kind of liked that. He said, 'You're not beautiful, by far, but we're gonna do this and we're gonna make it work and that's that.'"

"And you believed him?"

"I loved him as much as…I could possibly love someone at that time. He had the poise, the charm, the grace, the concentration, the nine yards plus the field goal, until he started hanging around biker bars and lesbian clubs."

"Daddy??"

"He was a very radical feminist."

"He always used to tell me, 'Life is a river. You can either drown, swim or find a boat.'"

"Yes," her mother said. "and he's in such a different mode these days. He's in more of a spiritual, sit back and chill, do some yoga and call it a night mode."

Boy, Becca thought, we have such layers of reality laying on top of nothing and legitimately there is no rhyme nor reason why things happen. "Well, thanks for the pep talk, Mom, gotta go."

"Ride long and hard, baby. We're red-liners, that's what we do."

"Will do."

Becca hung up, got into her old Suzuki Jeep. No insurance. Bad breaks. Drove to Venice beach, where she really began to dig her heels in and isolate herself.

She thought that sisterhood was powerful, until she realized that the ocean was incredibly loud and she couldn't hear a thing. She stopped, looked around and knew that she understood the world and she understood life.

a dream's gotta say something or it's not worth the trouble

I went to a shrink. He told me I was half crazy. I asked him for a prescription. He thought about it and gave me one.

But when I reached the pharmacy, I discovered the prescription had been written in invisible ink and I was shit out of luck.

So I went back to the shrink, but he had packed his bags and moved to Bali [so said the note on the door, anyway].

I was furious. I felt betrayed. Used. Like somebody had bored a hole into me with a hammer drill and taken my heart out and started playing dodge-ball with it.

I got so angry I went to Walmart and bought a single-shot short-barrel pump gun and took it home.

That night I slept with my gun, just like I saw those Marines in *Full Metal Jacket* sleep with theirs.

"Feels good," I said, as I drifted off to sleep.

I dreamed of some war-torn country. I saw guerilla fighters marching through the streets. They said they were from Ebinthia and that they belonged to the Antarctic Liberation Army.

I asked the leader if I could bum a cigar from him.

He just smiled and said, "I do not lend my cigars to men like you; I will sell you a cigar, though, for 7,171 wooden nickels."

I shook my head. "No, thanks. I can get 'em wholesale from the Ruskies."

The leader shrugged. "Have it your way," he said and he and his men continued marching toward The Fifty-Nine Years' Battle.

Now the scene shifted to a bungalow in West Hollywood. There were lemon trees in the back yard. I imagined one of the family members picking the lemons on the weekend and making Lemon Delight Pound Cake and

Lemon Meringue Pie. I wondered if there were small children living in the bungalow and if their parents had ever encouraged them to sell fresh-squeezed lemonade to their neighbors.

I imagined all kinds of idyllic, American scenes going on there. Barbeques, yard sales, reunions, potluck dinners.

"A home like that must have folk art wall hangings or paintings by Grant Wood and Frederic Remington and Norman Rockwell adorning the living room walls," I said.

I was about to walk up the cobblestone pathway leading to the front door when it suddenly swung open and a little old man with a rotund build and small-featured, delicate face appeared pointing a shotgun at me.

"You better git!" the old man said. "I got nothin' you want! Now git outa here!"

I raised both my hands above my head in surrender. "I don't want anything from you, sir. I was just admiring your home."

"Well, git goin' 'fore I call the cops."

"I was trying to envision who might live in such a beautiful home. And I love those lemon trees in your back yard."

"Yeah, well, you keep away from my lemon trees or I'll shoot ya."

"Sir, I didn't mean to..." I sighed quietly, lowered my hands and turned to leave. "I was just admiring your home," I said, and I walked away.

After that, I dreamed of being in a shadowy forest surrounded by a wispy fog.

A dark figure approached me.

"I am Arthur Rimbaud," said the figure, sipping from a reservoir glass filled with absinthe. "I understand you are one of the unhappy, fucked up tortured people."

I just stared at the twenty-one year old vagabond.

"You're the only one in charge of your happiness," said Rimbaud. "You can't depend on anyone else to make you happy. Paul Verlaine told me that shortly after he was released from prison. And then," Rimbaud chuckled derisively. "He converted to Catholicism. So much for his theory. Care for some hashish?"

I was about to say, "Is it blonde?" when I heard a phone ringing and my eyes snapped open.

I hate being wakened by the sound of a phone, I thought. *Or an alarm clock...or a barking dog...or a chirping bird...or a garbage truck...or a leaf blower...or a wood chipper...or a loud car muffler...*

By the time I finished listing all the things I hated being wakened by, the phone stopped ringing and I drifted back to sleep.

I dreamed I was being chased by a woman with delicate ears and large hands. She chased me through forests and deserts, over hills and across mountain ridges, into valleys, along riversides.

At one point she was barreling after me on the streets of San Francisco in a Pontiac LeMans; but she was no match for my Challenger R/T 440 Magnum and after some really impressive accelerating and cornering techniques, I was able to lose her near Haight and Ashbury streets.

The last thing I remember, I was on 101 North heading toward Napa County and badly wanting to get drunk on some of that Napa Valley vino when suddenly I heard that damn phone ringing again.

I decided to answer it.

It was Dad, calling from the Sunshine Home.

"I don't understand it," he said. "This Justin Bieber. Where's the talent? In the old days, Sinatra, Tony Bennett, Bing Crosby, Dean Martin, they were alone on stage with a microphone and it was just them singing. These new guys gotta have costume changes and laser lights and dancing and jumping and acrobats and strippers and fireworks and JumboTrons. It's phony!"

I'd had this conversation with my Dad at least four thousand times before but I was too tired to play devil's advocate with him this time, so I just let him vent.

"Those old crooners, they had personality. They didn't need all these fancy gimmicks to hide behind, y'understand. Jolson, you talk about an entertainer. Jolson had to project his voice to the back of the theater; he didn't even have a goddamn microphone. He did it all with his pipes. But this Justin Bieber. What's the attraction? What do people see in him? I guess I just don't understand it," and he hung up.

Laying my head down and staring at the ceiling, I thought, I'm in a really peculiar cycle right now.

I was awake but still very much asleep.

secrets and shame

She whispered to me, "You're the nicest guy I never got to know."

I knew exactly what she meant. I'd been less than forthcoming with certain information. Never knew which aspects of my personality to share with her. Just assumed the fewer the details, the better. Not that I was ashamed of myself. I can hear her say, "There exists within each of us a level of self-loathing." Mine wasn't severe, although I avoided mirrors and other people's eyes. I wasn't ex*actly* dissociative. I like to think I was involved on a *certain* level?

I had just recently begun to role-play, against type. We'd stand in groups of three and four, hands in our pockets, nodding slowly, swapping anecdotes with no pay-offs, saying, "Mm hmm, right," and then those long uncomfortable pauses, as long as our frown lines.

Then somebody would say, "Well, I think I'll go get some cocktail wieners and fruit punch," and we'd all scatter across the room, searching for our cliques. But all the cliques had gone home for the night, complaining of headaches and toothaches and early morning meetings with themselves.

I'd end up in the corner of a room or in a crawl space under some stair case with a pint of something my father used to drink before and after the Sabbath, reciting *Jonathan Livingston Seagull* to some young lady who'd just gotten over the flu or a manic episode.

I'd leave around two or three in the morning, alone, of course, and drive around town for a couple hours, circling the reservoir.

Who the hell knows why?

When I'd return home, I'd forget why I was there, then turn around and drive back into town where I'd park on Main Street by an expired parking meter, listening to the radio, and draining the battery.

Funny thing is, I never thought life was passing me by in those days.

You don't think about things like that because they're just too painful to think about.

So you think about other stuff instead, like babies and novels and the Bible and Disney and scrambled eggs and the Crusades and Batman and tequila and whatever else comes to mind.

Huh, I haven't thought about you lately.

Wonder why.

Probably because you don't love me anymore.

The day you stopped loving me was the day I began to forget.

without a light of doubt

I remember those days well. My doc began prescribing meds. Thorazine. For myself, I prescribed rotgut whiskey and bennies. Couldn't afford Martinis.

When I began losing my hair the following fall, I stopped shaving, downgraded my wardrobe, was suddenly on a first-name basis with shadows.

When I spoke, people would say, "What did you say?" at least fifty times. I'd tell them, "Don't worry about it, it's not important," and spend the rest of the day pouting.

The morning of the 5th I confessed to a woman on the third floor how much I enjoyed the poetry of Rod McKuen. When she refused to acknowledge me (I later learned the woman was stone deaf), I sunk into a profound depression, went back to my room, listened to "The Goodbye Girl" by David Gates a hundred and two times. Didn't make me feel any better.

When I awoke the next morning, I put on cheap sunglasses, went to church, pawned an electric guitar I'd won from a radio station autographed by Hanson, collected $25, went to the Waffle House, ordered a bowl of grits and a biscuit.

My waitress flirted with me. I asked her for her number. She just smiled and said, "You're adorable."

I didn't leave her a tip.

When I left, she tackled me in the parking lot.

"Sir, was there something wrong with the service?"

"I'm not working…I'm on a budget…I wish I could have tipped you, but…"

I broke down in tears.

She said, "I'm sorry. Don't worry about it." She reached into her pocket, offered me five dollars. "I know how it is being out of work."

"I can't take your money," I said.

"I want you to have it."

"You're very kind, but…"

She stashed the bill in my shirt.

"You're a true Christian," I said.

"I try to be."

"God bless you."

"He already has."

I steeled myself. "Can I call you sometime?"

"I'm sorry, I don't go out with unemployed guys," she said.

Crushed, I headed for the bus station, bought a one-way ticket to points unknown.

As I waited in the lobby, I was approached by a toothless woman in a Mother Hubbard dress.

"I was only thirty credits away from my degree in sociology when I had to leave school," she said with peanuts and beer on her breath. "I would have still been there, but they didn't allow you to stay when you're pregnant, and I was showing."

That's when I fell asleep and missed the bus.

But, I reminded myself, I've been doing that all my life.

let the sun set on this

I heard you when you said you don't like diamond cluster rings.

I heard you when you said grace before we ate our meal.

I heard you when you said you want to learn from me.

I heard you when you said you want to be pursued.

I heard you when you said you want to be able to submit yourself to me.

I heard you when you said you "got trust issues."

And I'll keep on hearing you until my ear drums are perforated.

Until those muscles near my eyes begin to twitch.

Until a thin fog develops in my eye, reducing my visibility.

Until the vertebrae in the base of my skull is numb.

And if you don't believe me, I've got the X-rays to prove just how much I really love you.

struggles and rebellion

They say good writing comes from the unconscious. Who knows where the hell this is coming from? This was told to me during a time when I was reading a lot of novelizations and books that relied heavily on dialogue to move the plot along.

I was writing myself in those days, still do, however, not as much, due to my lack of discipline, mostly in longhand, occasionally in shorthand, and in a pinch, long shorthand, and always by candlelight.

My characters were antiheroes, my plot was character-driven, my prose was external, like Chekhov's, my themes were theistic. I don't know why.

The first story I ever published was entitled "The Bored Tempestuous Heiress" and the opening sentence was: "It was a liverwurst sandwich and there was lipstick on the bread."

It was published by an underground zine called *Vacant Truth*, headquartered in the Marshall Islands. Its editor, an American Communist expatriate named Lefty Budupsker, wrote me personally: "Man, I dig this. It's got Marx written all over it. Freud, too. What are you, an idiot savant?"

Critics said my influences included Clifford Odets and Mad magazine, but in interviews, I was cheeky like Dylan, and told them I was actually influenced by God. They'd become visibly pale and ask me, "What gets you out of bed in the morning?" Wow. Basquiat had the best response to that question. He walked off camera and disappeared into his bedroom.

I actually enjoy interviews.

I usually communicate through sounds and nudges and stuff.

When they ask me about my childhood, I tell them it was a lot like Disneyland at four o'clock in the morning, and when they ask me to elaborate, I just tell them to go back and read their Kafka, then they'll understand.

the clichés stopped when i was drunk

I headed for The Open Flask, a little dive I frequent whenever I feel like overdosing on expired prescription medication.

The owner was a semi-acquaintance of mine named Zeke Balue, who'd served a couple duties in Nam and came home wondering who the hell he was.

As soon as he saw me, he smiled so big I could see his cleft pallet.

"How are ya, dude?" he said.

"Tired, tense, rather bitter, if you wanna know the truth," I said.

He knew just how to handle a self-pitying whack job like me.

"Pimm's Cup comin' right up," he said.

I sat my ass down at a lonely table in the corner, lit a cigarette, and stared into an unlimited expanse.

I tried to live in the present as much as I could and implement all those Buddhist principles into my daily life, but I wasn't always successful at doing that.

I really didn't have a handle on my thoughts.

Especially thoughts about my past.

They cropped up when I least expected them.

That was the trouble with thoughts.

They really pissed me off sometimes.

By the time Zeke brought my Pimm's Cup to me, I was daydreaming about angry sex with fragile women.

"Hope this'll help ya out," Zeke said.

"Zeke?" I said.

"Yaa?"

"Do ya remember your childhood?"

Zeke looked at me real puzzled like for a second. "Sure," he said.

"Remember all those nightmares you had?"

"Sure."

"Well, do you remember getting sudden head rushes whenever the air pressure changed, when the drinks were flowing and the drugs were epoch-making and your penis was raw from masturbating to MTV?"

This time Zeke didn't say "Sure."

In fact, he didn't say anything at all.

I think he was afraid to say anything.

Either that or I'd touched a nerve so deep in him that my question had left him totally paralyzed.

"I was just curious," I said, shrugging.

He half-smiled, but I could tell it was an effort for him. "No problem," he said. "Can I get'cha anything else?"

I looked at my Pimm's Cup. "Did you use lemonade or Ginger Ale this time?"

"Lemonade," he said. "Just like you like it."

"Good," I said. "Lemonade reminds me of the sun…You know, you're a good man, Zeke."

"Thank you," he said. "Anything else?"

I held out my hand.

We shook on something, but I'll be damned if I knew what it was.

Maybe on lost innocence or lost youth or something else that was lost.

Who knows?

I'm not all that good at finding the subtext in things, anyway.

That's probably why I write the kind of crap I write, which is nothing special.

I make a living at it, although I live in a tenement house on the lower east side and subsist on a diet of Cream of Wheat, ramen noodles, jelly doughnuts, and Boone's Farm apple wine.

Somebody once asked me if I considered myself a success.

That's one of those questions I hate.

And I told them how much I hated it.

That's probably why I don't have many friends.

I'm too honest.

Fuck 'em.

living is no newer

He said:

I don't really know

why I'm so sad.

She said:

It's because

you don't know

when to let go

of a tear.

He said:

I don't

understand my

sense of tragedy.

She said:

it's because

you got caught up

in the emergency

of your youth

rather than in the

safety of your death.

nothing to divide

In those days, the prevailing attitude toward Wiley Ouellette was that he was a fascist, not a socialist; although he swore up and down he was a-political, even at those city council meetings where he'd step up to the podium and talk about Eugene Debs, Joe Hill, and the Industrial Workers of the World.

In 1976 he was diagnosed with acid reflux, gingivitis and narcolepsy.

He couldn't have cared less; he'd been suffering from ulcers and conjunctivitis since he was eleven.

The year his father left him out of his will, he wrote a novella entitled "Victor the Hermit," about a nogoodnik who was the embodiment of kitsch.

When he went to the post office to mail out a hundred and two copies of his sublimation, the clerk behind the counter asked him, "Whaddaya, expecting immortality?"

"Just a good piece of ass," Wiley said.

As the rejection slips piled up, he used them to wallpaper his outhouse; it looked as though he was going to have to keep his night job as a remittance processor for the state's largest newspaper.

Following his ninety day probationary period, his supervisor called him into his office.

"Wiley, you're very quiet," said his supervisor. "I find there are two kinds of quiet people. The kind who are quiet, but you know they're happy. You're the other kind. I don't know if you're happy or not."

"Just know that I'm alive and well and living within my emotional means," Wiley said.

His supervisor just stared at him as a fire drill alarm interrupted their silence. "We'll finish this when we come back," he said.

As Wiley was standing in the parking lot with the rest of his coworkers, he noticed his supervisor lurking in the shade nipping from a flask.

Ten minutes later the security guards signaled an end to the fire drill and the employees were allowed to reenter the building.

When Wiley got back to his supervisor's cubicle, his supervisor wasn't there, so he went back to his desk, and emailed him:

"DON'T FIGHT PRESSURE WITH PRESSURE," he wrote. "YOU'LL ONLY END UP BROKEN-HEARTED."

After Wiley hit the 'send' button, he clocked out, walked to his car, drove to the library, where he checked out Adam Smith's *The Theory of Moral Sentiments* and Dr. Seuss' *The Lorax*.

a quiet neurotic bedtime

Nana stood by the picture window, staring out into the thickening fog.

"The day I was born," she said. "I'm sure I sighed in despair…I'm certain I did."

I heard a door close behind me. It was my mother, lying in bed without an expression.

The wind started to pick up. So did the rain.

Nana said she was going out to visit Papa, who was buried in the back yard underneath the old oak tree.

"But it's storming out," I said.

She shrugged, "It doesn't matter."

She picked up her Bible and walked outside, without a raincoat or an umbrella.

I decided to join her.

As we stood under that oak tree, (I noticed the caterpillars had just begun to feed on the newly emerging leaves), she read from the Book of Job. And when she got to the part where God let Job know He was only testing him and that he was going to reward Job with twice the wealth and more children, Nana just shook her head and said, "I can't figure out why this ending pisses me off so much!"

We went back inside.

In the corner of the living room, she lit some birthday candles. "I don't have any yortsayt candles."

I bowed my head.

She recited a blessing in Hebrew, then a proverb in English. "The spirit of man is the candle of The Lord."

Meanwhile, my mother awoke from a nightmare, came into the living room, rubbing her eyes.

She looked at Nana, yawned, belched, lit a Pall Mall, and said, "Mom, that was a terrific speech."

That's when the power went out.

We stood by the light of those birthday candles, in dead silence, sizing up the dark and shying away from pushing ourselves to the limit.

this bewailing cry

Phone rings, somebody on the other end wants to know when I'm coming to visit them.

I'm so distracted I mutter, "Haven't been myself lately."

"Hmm? What did you say?"

"Nothing," I say, wiping sweat from my brow.

The caller waits for me to say something else, but I don't, which makes the caller very uncomfortable, and they finally break the silence by saying, "Still working through some things, are you?"

"Always," I say.

Another pause and another numb feeling.

"Sounds like I got you at a bad time," the caller says, and I confirm this by intoning, "Mmmm…"

"Well, let me let you go. I'll talk to you later."

The caller hangs up, but I keep the receiver to my ear until the busy signal stops and I'm transferred to a recorded message that says, "If you'd like to make a call, please hang up and try again. If you need help, hang up and then dial your operator."

I need help, I think, *but not from you.*

Then I remember something a friend whispered to me the previous week.

"You're starting to like your solitude a little too much."

"What do you mean," I say.

"Time to venture out," says my friend, pointing to my head. "And become a living, moving thing again."

A fleeting moment passes and that phrase, "living, moving thing," is swiftly distributed across both hemispheres of my brain; and although on the surface it sounds a bit naive and corny, it gets at the truth of something and goes directly to the core of my psyche, deeply affecting me.

She's absolutely right.

My life has become a quick moving river and I'm just trying to stay afloat and not hit any sharp rocks or uneven river beds. I'm a bit angry with my life, myself. Always verging on feeling sorry for myself. Doing things for all the wrong reasons. I need to restore to me something that was very important to me when I was a kid. Something I've lost. Or lost sight of or the grasp of.

I need to find a form for my experience, but I'm sure what to write about.

For years I've bisected the psyche of the man with the fierce moral sensibility who can't make any peace with the world and covered my canvases with the long, emotional colors of all those lost people who find themselves by recognizing their love for one another, but I've never been able to find the precise rising line of conflict and resolution to those themes.

Maybe because I've compromised my form and am no longer capable of serious introspection.

I've become another 21st century working class antihero trying to come to grips with the reality of my own life; too exhausted to develop anything more than the callouses on my finger tips from all that wild and uncontrolled typing.

"Getting stuck is what makes us not move," says my friend. "You've got to move into a different place and find what it is you want to write about."

I pause. Then somewhat self-mocking say, "I used to want to write about how we all have to work to find the best in ourselves and others. How there should be less suffering and more humanity, liberty, equality and peaceful coexistence. But that's just a very pleasant fiction. There's no way to follow that tale to its end. You can never solve the moment when you write about things like that."

Sighing with sentiment, my friend says, "Your fantasies have lapsed into frustration."

That's when I begin to wonder just how far down this brown-eyed troubadour can go.

over the dark bay

I got high, looked to the sky, saw my mother cry and the sun refused to shine.

The skies turned black and it began to snow.

I made love to a girl named Orion.

When I looked into her eyes I saw stars shining.

I kissed her shin and she grinned.

Tears rolled off her face and moistened her breasts.

I closed my eyes.

I saw children smiling, flying high above the clouds, chasing rainbows, dancing on the moon.

They whispered my name, offered me sweet rain and chocolate stars which are by far my favorite indulgence.

They took me by the hand, sprinkling me with dust from the land.

I was drowsy but I could stand.

The children formed a circle around me and began to sing:

"A bird's wing in a sling never feeling a thing as long as it's worshipping."

I watched the moon; it looked like a Botox-smile in the sky.

I asked them why, they just sighed. They were busy feeling dizzy and thirsting for more; one eye on the door, the other on the score.

I was floating through space watching my face glancing at a foreign place. Images flashing across the sky: Colored balloons, a mile-long parade, apples in the shade, frowning clowns, deserted towns, pretty women singing soft songs, blowing kisses to passersby and Orion, my love, waving goodbye to her high-flying guy.

fifty-five years too late for the village thing

I

It was the end of a long day. And alcohol was involved. I decided to move to New York City because I'd seen pictures of the Statue of Liberty and Lady Liberty just looked so nurturing and welcoming and approachable; just the kind of woman I needed in my life at that time.

I took a bus.

Shared a seat with a woman named Hazel who had just left her husband.

"He forgot how fond I am of packed suitcases," she said. "So off I went."

She was curious about my Star of David tattoo. "Are you Jewish?"

"Yes, ma'am."

She immediately began listing every Jewish person she ever knew. "Do you attend synagogue?"

"No, ma'am."

This concerned her. "You're still of the faith, aren't you?"

"Yes, ma'am. I'm very spiritual."

She nodded. Slowly. Appeared frustrated because she couldn't read me. Badly wanted to confront me on a few issues. Didn't have the chutzpah.

I fell asleep.

Woke up in Yonkers.

Hazel was REM-ing. Lightly snoring. Clutching a book called "Mammals of Uruguay."

II

I stepped over a body my first day there.

Walked up on an abandoned birthday cake day two; the candles were still lit.

Day three a clown sat Shiva in Madison Square Park.

Day four a beat poet muttered under a yawning awning, "Too much, man, too much."

Day five. Well, let's just say day five was one of those incredibly, unholy days when things get so bad that you have to self-medicate.

A certain amount of physical coordination was required on day six, Fortunately I was able to do this while lying face-down in a puddle of fortified wine.

On day seven somebody handed me a loaded Glock and perhaps it was a bad idea, but it felt good, my friend. It felt really good.

Look, all I'm saying is, I don't think I did anything fundamentally wrong. And that's all I'm saying. And that's without counsel.

adult reflections on childhood

It was another washed-out blue Monday.

I'd slept miserably.

That damn recurrent dream about being swathed in the snug-fitting clothing of my family's dark secrets.

Father, wall-eyed, dime cigar between his false teeth, alcohol blackouts, sleep walking.

Mother, blank-eyed, haunted by a past involving medication, always telling us "God will be there to take care of you."

Sister, sad-eyed, always walking through doorways crying, drinking to act normal, addicted to childhood memories.

Brother, black-eyed, a little gutted, scratching and clawing, trying to do everything he can.

And me, glaze-eyed, itinerant, bohemian at sixteen, another mysterious hitchhiker on a deserted road.

Wiping the nightmare from my eyes, I got out of bed, lit a cigarette, fetched the newspaper.

The news was typical for a washed-out blue Monday.

Epic stories of suffering and endurance, repressed weaknesses, shortcomings, instincts, the structure of psychosis, ego and the self. Men and women struggling with the meaning and purpose of life, searching for their authentic selves in an inauthentic world. Editorials attempting to expose fascistic social repression. Columns exploring morality through a metaphysical framework. And a couple of uplifting quotes from the class valedictorian.

"To be here now, alive in the world as it is rather than as we imagine it to be"

"The truth about any choice that we make is that those choices will resonate throughout the rest of our lives."

Such startling depth and universal pathos.

My day could now begin.

catching heartbreaking glimpses of our lives

i

Sitting at my desk, staring blankly at the empty page in a typewriter. I light a bidi, pour a drink, scratch an itch, rub the tension from my face, look out the window, stare back at the empty page, rub my hands together, take a deep breath, expel it loudly, smoke, sip the drink, stare at the letters on the typewriter, point one by one to the letters P-O-E-T. Finally, frustrated, I type the following word in caps with one finger: "TIME".

ii

Sitting at my desk, staring at the word "TIME" I typed the night before. Stare out the window, run my fingers across my scalp, belch, get up, drop to the floor to do a series of clapping push-ups, then rise to my feet and do about ten jumping jacks.

iii

Sitting at my desk, my right elbow leaning on the desk top. Take a drag from the bidi, set it in a tin ash tray, look at the word "TIME" on the paper, wait, then begin typing the following sentence: "Now is the time for all good men to come to the aid of their country." I stop, read the sentence, begin typing the same sentence again on the next line. Halfway through, I recall an army recruiting office where an army recruiter smiles wide as he hands me a pen so I can sign a contract. Then a hand stamps an official document with the phrase: "UNFIT FOR SERVICE."

iv

Lying in bed, unable to sleep. Look at the clock which reads 3:45 AM. I sigh. See the image of me at age 10 holding a stack of books in my lap which my father has advised me to read.

I glance at a few of the titles: The Old Testament, The New Testament, Plato's *Dialogues*, Aristotle's *Book IV of Nicomachean Ethics*, Lao Tzu's Tao *Te Ching*, J.D. Salinger's *The Catcher in the Rye*.

I look up at my father, quite puzzled.

"Your assignment," says my father. "Is to write a two-hundred page report on each of those books and deliver it to me on the day you turn 30."

I am totally overwhelmed.

"Any questions?" says my father.

v

On the morning of my 30th birthday, my father, overwhelmed by a coughing fit, is rushed to the hospital, and dies later that day, without ever having read my two-hundred page book report.

vi

Sitting at my desk, a lighted bidi dangling from my lips, it finally dawns on me: I didn't read all those books for him; I read them for myself. And I didn't write that two-hundred page book report for him, either.

vii

Sitting at my desk, concluding a big yawn, staring at the word "TIME" I typed the night before, I begin typing.

"The Poet runs down a long, dark, narrow corridor, sweating profusely, anxiously looking back at where he's been and quite uncertain of where he's going; yet he continues to run in search of the finish line."

ABOUT THE AUTHOR

PHILIP GABER is a freelance writer. He was raised and educated in Connecticut, traveled around a bit, worked at a seemingly random series of occupations, spends the majority of his day attempting to reconcile differences between his conscious and subconscious. In his spare time he tries not to drift around his community as an invisible spirit or juggle more than a handful of moral dilemmas at a time. His first book, *Between Eden and the Open Road* was published in 2012. For the past thirteen years he has worked as an instructor for an organization whose vision is for all people in its region to have the opportunity to develop to their fullest potential through family-sustaining employment. He currently lives in North Carolina.

www.ingramcontent.com/pod-product-compliance
Lightning Source LLC
Chambersburg PA
CBHW060746180626
46818CB00002B/471